Ashley

I Hope you enjoy the adventures of Harry Caine!

Dane Shaffer
10/8/05

A HARRY CAINE Mystery

Published by Alabaster Books
North Carolina

This is a work of fiction. Names, characters, places, and incidents either are the product of the author's imagination or are used fictitiously and any resemblance to actual persons, businesses, events, or locales is coincidental.

Copyright 2003 by David Shaffer
All rights reserved. Printed in the United States of America. No part of this book may be reproduced in any manner whatsoever without written permission except in the case of brief quotations embodied in critical articles and reviews.

Published by Alabaster Books
P.O. Box 401
Kernersville, North Carolina 27285

Book design by D.L.Lee
Cover concept and graphic art by
Jim Shaffer, Gainesville, Florida

First Edition

ISBN:0-9725031-6-1

Library of Congress Control
Number:2003114609

ACKNOWLEDGMENTS

The author wishes to acknowledge
the invaluable assistance of the
following people:

Mary Shaffer; Jim Shaffer, Frances Shaffer;
the bi-weekly critique of the
Triad Writer's Roundtable members:
Dixie Land Jakubsen, Larry Jakubsen,
Joanne Clarey, Kathy Fisher, John Staples,
Chuck Smithers, Lynette Hampton,
Elizabeth Hedgecock, and Helen Goodman;
San Francisco's Anna Chavez; Ayn Ferrante;
Detective Captain Gary Hastings,
Greensboro, N.C. Police Department;
Capt. Dick Townley, airline pilot (Ret.);
Secret Service Agent Dan Dlusneski,
U.S. Secret Service Public Affairs Dept.,
Washington, D.C.

Dedicated to those
Private Investigators across America
who, in addition to making a living,
contribute their efforts to
the maintenance of
a moral society.

1

The day I was dreading was here. The boat repair was finished and I couldn't cover the cost. It wasn't a surprise. I'd known it from the day I let them haul Anthem out of the water. I was so focused on making my dream come true that I convinced myself that getting the boat fixed was the most important thing to do. Paying the bill would somehow take care of itself. The last ten days had been building to this point, and hearing the sudden pounding on the side of my boat, coupled with someone shouting my name, was like the ending of a ten-day crescendo.

I came out of the cabin onto the boat's warm wood deck. It was Earl, the yard foreman of the Daytona Boat Yard. Earl's usual jovial demeanor had given way to a concerned look.

"Hi Harry, hate to be the bearer of bad news. Here's your bill." Earl's lean, vertically-lined face and his serious, yet relaxed, manner gave the impression that he only spoke the truth. During my stay at the boat yard we discussed how boats should be built. He thought Anthem had been built right. We got along.

"What's the damage?"

"Read it and weep, man."

I took the envelope from Earl.

"Let me know if you need anything else, Harry. You can stay tied up here for another day and then you'll have to move."

I thanked him for his quality workmanship and went below to read the bill.

An electric shock went through my stomach when I saw the total amount due. Five thousand five hundred and thirty-three dollars. My net worth consisted of the boat, and fifteen hundred dollars in cash hidden behind a piece of mahogany at the bottom of the bookcase in the main cabin.

An hour after receiving the invoice, I went to the controller's office at the front entrance to the boat yard. The only thing I could think of was that I would do whatever it takes in order not to lose the boat. The posted boat-yard policy stated that the yard had the right to hold the boat for ninety days, and if the bill was not paid, they could sell it and take their share out of the proceeds. My morale was sliding faster than a penny stock during a depression.

The molded piece of concrete tucked under the front eaves of the wood building housing the boat yard offices was dated seventy years ago. The building looked as though it had been heavily used every day of its life. Walking up to the office, the unpainted, weathered-wood stairs creaked like an old boat.

The second floor of the building was one room the size of the perimeter of the building. The room had obviously been used to produce and repair large sails. The main worktable was still in place. The sewing tools were still in the tool bin at the end of the large table. The rest of the room was empty and smelled of the dark linseed oiled floor, the kind that you sprinkle sawdust on before sweeping up. One end of the sail loft was walled-off into an open outer office occupied by a secretary, and an inner office whose door displayed a sign with white letters on a black plastic background that read, "Controller." The name, "Moshe Zucker," appeared in smaller capitals below it.

The secretary was long in the tooth; about five foot five, one-hundred-ten pounds with dyed-red hair. Her pale complexion, red lipstick and pageboy with bangs coupled with the pink polyester dress made her look like an albino on holiday. A nameplate placed at the front edge of her desk read Ricki Burkholder. It was the neatest thing in the office. Worn manila folders lay in a jumbled mess behind the nameplate. A small, dark, wood table in one corner of her area held a glass coffeepot showing various shades of brown. A few stained coffee mugs sat on the same table among spill streaks that had made their way from the tabletop, through all the decorative trim and brass handles, to the floor. Ricki Burkholder smiled, showing lipstick-smudged teeth.

What the hell was I doing here? The ambiance, coupled with the image of Ricki Burkholder, framed the question. I felt like the guy who couldn't pay for his meal at a restaurant and wound up washing dishes. It wasn't my style. I thought of the day I gave notice to my boss and he immediately let me know that anyone who would quit the job I held for the past two years was crazy. His last words were, "Don't forget your name plate, Caine. And by the way, Harry, if you ever need another government job, try the weather bureau."

As amusing as his comment might have been, another government job was not in my plans. I would be self-employed, just as I had been for fifteen years prior to taking the D.C. job. The question was whether or not I would be self-employed as a licensed private investigator, as I was, in California, before the move.

The what-he-thought-was-funny remark about my name had just been the latest in a long string of questionable comments on that subject. Even though the name might be comical, it's my name, and I'm not all that funny. A lot of guys have found that out. I'm six one, medium build with a square face and dark hair. That's what you see on the outside. Inside is a different story; some anxieties, a gall bladder that is slowly heading south, and knees that have tendon problems from a twenty-year-old sledding accident. Ricki Burkholder's smudged lipstick came into focus.

"What do you need, Honey?" Ricki Burkholder asked.

"I want to talk to Mr. Zucker. Is he available, or do I need an appointment?" Ricki Burkholder's eyes momentarily focused on my crotch.

"What's it about?"

"My yard bill for repairs on Anthem."

"Yeah, he can talk to you now. Follow me." Ricki Burkholder's ass had melted into her thighs some years ago.

Zucker was an unkempt little guy in his late thirties or early forties. His narrow face came to a point under black hair that was slicked down and combed straight back in a mob-do. He was wearing a rumpled white dress shirt with a tie whose small greasy-looking knot was off-center.

He looked like the kind of person I wouldn't voluntarily talk with.

Zucker was sitting behind his desk, partially buried in invoices and ledgers. A threadbare rug with an oriental design in front of the desk was bunched up on one end. It felt like a bed sheet under my feet. The wood slat Venetian blinds were open enough to highlight a thick layer of dust on each slat. On the wall behind his desk, a large frame held a matted, sun-faded and dusty, Harvard Business School diploma.

"What the hell's your problem?"

"I'm Harry Caine. I own Anthem. I'd like to talk to you about my yard bill. I want to trade my labor for a portion of the bill."

"God! You boat bums are all the same, just enough money to get yourself a boat and then think you won't need any more. What's with you guys? The boat will never need repairs? You'll just sail through life eating fish and looking in sympathy at the rest of us idiots who think we have to work for a living?"

Zucker had sharply focused eyes that were staring at me. I felt the blood rush to my face. The problem I always have with this type of confrontation is that I feel above being talked to that way, even though I knew he was speaking the truth. I make it a practice to yield to what I consider truth and I've taken a lot of crap doing it. I made an exception in his case. I took two quick steps forward and grabbed Zucker by his tie and pulled. His face hit the desk hard. The ink blotter pad on the desk began to get dark and wet, starting at Zucker's nose.

"Look Zucker, I came here to see how I could pay you. Work, trading personal property, whatever. Now let's get down to it, and don't think about calling anybody in here or I'll break your neck. Whataya say we make a deal?"

I felt good. The controller's piercing look changed to one of submission.

Zucker straightened up, grabbed a handkerchief out of his back pocket and plugged his nose with it.

"O.K., so you're tough. I know a lot tougher where I come from and you're damn lucky I'm not in the mood to call in a favor."

This guy probably grew up having his arrogant attitude rewarded by parents who thought he could do no wrong. I wondered what had happened to him. He looked very permanent here and here was not where a Harvard Business School grad should be.

"Well, you wanted to talk about your yard bill, so talk." Zucker was almost back to the way he was when I walked into his office, minus a shade of arrogance.

"To make a long story short, I don't have the fifty-five hundred I owe you. I'd like to trade labor, or anything that you can suggest that lets me keep my boat." It was a statement, not a request.

"Hey, business is business, I'll forget about your bad temper. The boat stays at the yard for ninety days and if you don't have the bill paid by then, we auction it off. Those are the rules. Live with 'em."

"Okay, let me put it this way. Do you know a way I can earn five grand in ninety days?"

Zucker looked interested,

"What do you do for a living? I mean before you got boat fever."

It took me about two microseconds to mentally review my work life. The only thing I had ever done was investigative work. It was what I know how to do well, and the work that gives me a feeling of pride. All my clients get the very best I have to offer. I can't say that about many PI's I've worked with. I think our professional status in society is still somewhere below waterfront bartender, but improving.

I owe my success as an investigator to the fact that I'm an all-American looking guy with above average intelligence who looks professional and non-threatening. And by success I mean making enough money to pay the rent, put food on the table and have a little left over.

My years of experience as a private investigator taught me how to find someone who had disappeared; locate someone's hidden assets; conduct background checks without getting sued in the process; catch insurance cheaters, and a variety of other assignments for attorneys and insurance companies. I couldn't see how I could tie my investigative experience in with boat-yard work that paid minimum wage. With expenses taken out it would take a year to get the boat out of hock.

Answering Zucker's question, I said, "I'm a California licensed private investigator and I decided I needed a career change. I was burned out after fifteen years of running my own investigative agency in the San Francisco Bay Area and a divorce during my last year in California didn't help. I applied and eight months later was accepted for a position with the Bureau of Industry and Security. It's a group inside the Department of Commerce in Washington, D.C. I thought the job was going to be a little more exciting than it turned out to be. Going to work in a little cubicle sifting through export shipping documents, trying to find companies that were violating the ban on shipment of electronic components to foreign countries, was more than boring."

"Sounds like you didn't ask enough questions about the job or about yourself before making the change." Zucker stated, judgmentally.

"Yeah, well I wouldn't talk. Look what happened to you." I said as I swept my arm across the office. Zucker's expression turned sour.

"We're not talking about me, hotshot. I'm not the one with a money problem." Zucker gave me a smug look. "You were saying?" Zucker's eyebrows arched, prompting me to continue.

"Like I was saying, I was bored with the job. I had trouble staying awake by mid-afternoon every day. I thought the job would fire me up but it didn't. It just made me realize that what I had really needed was a long vacation. I started building Anthem during my second month on the job. The idea was to sail off to some island and never look back. It took me two years and about all my savings by the time I launched the boat in the Anacostia River, near downtown Washington D.C."

Zucker looked amused and asked, "Why the name Anthem?"

I had named her Anthem in tribute to an author who influenced me during my college years, but I wasn't going to share that with Zucker. Instead I said, "Hey, it's a name. What difference does it make why I chose it?"

I continued by pouring out my work history hoping to give him five grand worth of relevant experience. Zucker, dabbing at his nose with the handkerchief, didn't blink.

"So what happened to your boat that you picked us to be the suckers?"

"I came down the Intracoastal Waterway. A drawbridge tender at Ormond Beach decided to close the bridge before I could get through. I didn't make the 180-degree turn before going outside of the channel boundaries and running aground. I had damage to the rudder and rudder shaft, and needed to be hauled out to get it fixed.

Your boat yard was the nearest facility and that's where the Coast Guard took me."

After a few moments of silence Zucker said, "Actually, there is a possibility. Get back to me in the morning. I'll see what I can do. Maybe you'll get lucky."

With that I left Zucker's office, smiled at Ricki Burkholder on my way out and watched her eyes go to my crotch. I felt taller than when I came in. Some of the pressure was gone and I splurged for a bottle of wine. The world didn't look quite so gray.

I slept about two hours that night and felt weary when I opened my eyes at first light the next morning. I was anxious about going to see Zucker. If he had something that could make me five grand in ninety days, why would he be shuffling invoices at a broken down boat yard with his Harvard degree hanging on the wall? Everyone is motivated by a few primary needs, the first being to stay alive, and then comes money, sex and power in some order. The boat yard was just a place to stay alive.

2

I didn't want to appear overly anxious so I waited until 10:00 a.m. before going to Zucker's office. Ricki Burkholder saw me coming across the old sail loft and smiled her long-tooth smile.

"He's expecting you, go on in." She said with a grin just before her eyes headed south. As I entered Zucker's office he was talking on the phone with his back toward me.

"Don't worry, I'm a good judge of character. I'll call you after it's fixed." He put the old-fashioned phone receiver in its cradle and turned to face me.

"Looks like I can help you out, Caine." This was said as though our relationship was boss to junior apprentice. Guess who junior was. Many years of dealing with people who lie taught me that when a stranger tells me he can help me out, it always means that I can help him out, at more cost to me than to him.

"Well, that's why I'm here, Zucker. Let's hear it."

"A business acquaintance of mine needs an experienced person like you to courier some valuable merchandise from here to California. The merchandise has to be delivered tomorrow, Wednesday."

I felt a sense of relief that he didn't offer me a boat-yard-labor job. Now we were back on my ground. I had done a few courier jobs as a PI. My heart was pounding a little when I said, "What's the merchandise you want me to carry and where, exactly, do I carry it?"

"Personal treasures, jewels and other small art objects. For security purposes, the owner wants the stuff delivered personally. No contraband. No drugs. No sniffing dogs. No problems. A delivery job by someone who has the right background and someone the owner can trust to be motivated to get the job done without any problems. Zucker paused for a moment, appearing to think about what he was about to say. He continued. "The objects are packaged in five wood containers each weighing about sixty pounds. Each container has a handle for carrying. The containers will be checked as additional baggage on Delta's 10:00 p.m. flight to San Francisco, with a stop in Dallas. The baggage claim tickets will be part of the ticket folder. They'll be ready for you to pick up any time after 8:00 p.m. today at the Delta counter. The containers will be checked from Daytona Beach to San Francisco. After picking them up in San Francisco, you'll deliver them to an address in Palo Alto. You'll get a signed receipt for the delivery., and then take the signed receipt to a person at an address in Mountain View. I assume you know where both places are. All the instructions have been written and will be waiting for you with your ticket, at the Delta counter. Your job is complete after you deliver the receipt in Mountain View, and you'll be able to pick up your boat any time after that."

The instructions were clear. It sounded as though Zucker had done this before. Zucker then added, "I left the return flight open for your convenience. In return for your services, your yard bill will be zeroed out. I'll front you five hundred against expenses, and when the job is finished you're free to take your boat with no balance due. Questions?"

"One question and one requirement. When do I get the five hundred? And I want to open the containers before taking the flight."

"You get the five hundred right now if you accept the job. You won't be allowed to open the containers. The owner doesn't want to compromise the security of the merchandise from the time he packs it until it reaches its destination. You'll have to trust me. You can balance that trust on your need to get your boat back."

"I'll think on it and let you know at noon."

"Let me put it this way Caine, it's a one time offer. Take it or lose your boat." Restraining myself from attacking, I said, "I'll be back at noon."

Zucker nodded okay to the noon meeting.

It was a 'no brainer' that the offer involved something illegal. People just don't pay that kind of money for delivering a few containers of prized possessions. After deliberating with myself for a few hours, my survival instinct outweighed all other concerns.

I met with Zucker at noon and presented him with the one condition that stood in the way of me taking the job. I wanted him to give me a copy of the boat repair invoice, marked paid in full, before I left for California. After ten minutes of haggling I finally agreed to accept the assignment and he agreed to give me a written statement that the invoice for the boat repair would be marked paid-in-full, after I completed the courier job. He reluctantly wrote the short note, dated and signed it, and slammed it into my hand.

He went over the details of picking up the plane tickets, the baggage claim tickets, and the written instructions. I planned on being at the Daytona Beach airport several hours early, hoping to spot the person who would check in the five, sixty-pound containers. In this kind of game, you keep your eye on the ball and who had it last.

Zucker gave me five hundred in cash for two days expenses. I returned to my boat, which was now docked at the boat-yard fuel pier. After a leisurely afternoon of lunch, a book and a doze, I checked the dock lines for chaffing gear placement, made sure the electrical connection to the 110-volt power was securely in place, checked the position of the fenders, and closed the water intake valve to the engine. I threw some underwear, socks, a pair of khaki pants, a shirt, shaving kit, note pad, a couple of pens and an old San Francisco Bay Area Thomas Guide into my duffel bag. The worn, brown-leather duffel bag was like an old friend from my days as a California PI. The bag was missing one item that I would normally carry on an out-of-town assignment. My laptop computer. I had dropped it in into the Anacostia River during my move onto the boat. As a reflex, I dove into that biological stew and retrieved it. It never worked again, and even though I promised myself to try and save the hard drive, I never made the attempt. I figured I'd never use it again, going into the life I had planned to live. I was going to replace it, but as the boat building progressed, my spending priorities didn't include a new laptop. After locking the cockpit-hatch-cover, I left the boat and used the public phone on the fuel dock to call a cab to take me to the airport.

3

It was 6:00 p.m. when the cab dropped me off at the airport: two hours earlier than I planned. The sky was dark and clear to the east, becoming lighter at the western horizon where there was still a streak of indigo holding back the darkness. It was sixty-five degrees. All in all, a good evening for a take-off and I had two "take-offs" ahead of me. I always tell myself I'm never going to fly again. If I can't get there by car in the required time I won't go. But, when it comes to doing a job that involves flying; I always manage to get through it.

I stationed myself in an outer fringe seat of the open bar tacitly announcing that I didn't want a drink, just a place to sit. The bar was in the far corner of the terminal building and provided an unobstructed view of the Delta ticket counter across a wide expanse of white, speckled, gleaming tile floor. The airport was nearly empty. There was one uniformed ticket agent at the Delta counter and two people at the counter next door to Delta. This was probably one of the few remaining international airports where you walked out of the terminal onto an asphalt plane-docking area and up a set of portable stairs into the plane.

I mindlessly stared at a re-run of the 'Dating Game', while keeping one eye on the ticket counter. The bar clientele, all five of them, were guessing who would be chosen for the date. Heavy stuff.

At 6:30 p.m., a delivery service man in a khaki work uniform wheeled in the five packages on a piano dolly. I watched him check the packages according to the written instructions he was reading to the ticket-clerk. He paid cash for the extra baggage charge and gave the ticket-clerk an envelope. I left the bar area and walked outside to the curb before he finished checking the packages in. The only vehicle at the curb was a Ford cargo van with the name of Scarapelli Express of Jacksonville written on its side. While I was looking at the van, the driver returned, shoving paper into his shirt pocket. As the van drove away, I noted the Fernandina Beach address written on the back of the truck just below the company motto, *"We carry anything anywhere and get it there yesterday."*

I returned to the terminal and stopped by the Delta ticket counter. I showed the clerk my photo ID and asked for my pre-paid ticket for the 10:00 p.m. flight to San Francisco. Zucker had purchased the tickets through a travel agency, paid by credit card, and instructed the agency to deliver them to the Delta counter. The clerk checked me in, handed me my ticket folder with the baggage claim tickets stapled to the inside front cover along with an envelope that the deliveryman had left for me. He said that the delivery service had just checked my packages through to San Francisco. I asked if the containers seemed to be sturdy and was told that they were very solid and that each container had weighed fifty-nine pounds.

Everything seemed to be okay. It looked like a legitimate delivery service. There was nothing to do now except to wait for the plane and the take-offs. I considered that I was being too suspicious. Maybe I just lucked-out by being in the right place at the right time with the right background. Yeah, right. Right now my place was to wait until the flight boarded at 9:40 p.m. The thought of spending the next two hours doing nothing but watching TV, nursing one, maybe two martinis, and possibly meeting an interesting woman, was not unpleasant.

I sat down at one of the small, round, blacktop-tables in enough light to read the contents of the envelope. The carpet quieted the background noise. I waited for the approaching waitress to take my order before opening the envelope. I had a sudden feeling of deja vu. The bar, the typical travelers, the waitress with the straight black skirt, white blouse and piled-up blonde hair, made up the same scene you would see at the airport in Chicago, Los Angeles, New York, Boston or San Francisco.

I opened the letter, which was unsigned and had no return address. It stated that the five packages were to be delivered at 10:00 a.m. on 24 November to a Theodore Martin at 17000 Gorge Drive in Palo Alto, California. I was instructed to get a receipt for the delivery from Martin. When I read the address and name of the person to whom I would be giving the signed receipt, my eyes bugged out. Daniel Nelson, Esq. I knew the guy! Nelson and I went to law school together in 1975. We had hired on with a local private investigative agency to learn how the private sector conducted investigations. I liked the work so much that I dropped out of law school, and stayed with the PI firm for the next five years, which was how long it took to accumulate the required six-thousand working hours of experience. I applied and received my California PI license and went out on my own. Nelson went on to finish his law degree at a back-east university. He had dated my sister, Susan, for a while before going east to finish his degree. I had done a few investigations for him over the years. It had been six or seven years since I last saw him. Small world. I was sure he would tell me what I had delivered to Martin.

  The plane boarded promptly at 9:40 p.m. My window seat was in a three-across row where the other two seats were not sold. A good start. I watched the remaining luggage being loaded onto the plane and realized that I was looking at my five packages. Nothing unusual about them except when the loader picked each package from the tram to put on the conveyor belt, his forearms and biceps strained under the weight.

  The plane was half-full. Probably normal for the red-eye. The take-off was uneventful even though you couldn't tell it by looking at the grip I laid on the arms of my seat. The flight attendant sensed my uneasiness, as she was passing my row.

  "We'll be in level flight in just a moment and the Captain says that it will be a smooth flight all the way to Dallas."

  Hearing those words from the flight attendant, I felt some tension leave my body. "Did he say anything about the weather going from Dallas to San Francisco?"

  "No, but the weather is fairly stable across the entire country right now. Mid-November is a good time of year to fly and this is actually a good time of day to fly across the country."

I thanked her and ordered a couple of beers to go with the honey coated nuts that were bound to arrive shortly.

I pulled off my coat thinking I probably shouldn't have brought it. The long-sleeved, dark-blue rayon shirt would last me the whole trip. On the other hand, I could never tell when I might have to look professional. Professional attire, a daily shave and shined shoes will get you by in situations where looks count more than content. I stored the coat in the upper luggage compartment, grabbed a few chiclet-sized pillows and settled in just as the flight attendant returned with my two beers, and nuts.

I finished the beers, felt appropriately groggy, and took a nap. I was awakened by the captain announcing that we were making our approach to the Dallas airport.

The flight from Dallas to San Francisco was smooth and the night slipped away. The drone of the engines created a sense of well-being that I hadn't felt for sometime. With flights like this, I could lose my fear of flying.

4

I left the plane and walked to the baggage-claim area at the San Francisco airport. It took seven minutes for the first bag to surface from the underground into the cold florescent light of the baggage carousel area. The five heavy packages popped up, one-by-one, and I lifted each by its handle and placed them side-by-side, on the floor, like five oversized briefcases. Each package appeared to be about two-and-one-half feet square and four inches thick. I laid a twenty on a baggage porter who rounded up a mobile carrier large enough to carry the five containers. He wheeled the loaded cart to the arrival passenger pickup area in front of the building and with much exertion loaded the containers into a cab using the trunk and rear seat space. I climbed into the front seat and told the driver to go to the California Hotel on El Camino Real in Palo Alto. He looked happy to get the thirty-five mile fare.

The California Hotel is a motor hotel. This simplified the problem of getting the containers into the room. The driver grunted respectfully at the load and received an extra ten spot for effort. It was now 3:15 a.m. on Wednesday the 24th. The room had a fresh look and the big bed was soft. I placed a wake-up call for 8 a.m. and lay down on the bed. The next thing I was aware of was the telephone ringing.

The morning was cool, cloudless and crisp, the kind of weather that entices people to come to northern California. I rented a full-sized car from the Hertz desk in the lobby, loaded the five containers into the car and went across the street to a local greasy-spoon. I could see the car while I ate, which kept me honest about not letting the containers out of my sight. My usual breakfast of sausages, eggs, and fried potatoes hit the spot.

Getting into the car, I pulled the Thomas guide for the Bay Area counties from my duffel bag and located Gorge Drive.

Page Mill Road meanders up the eastern side of the Coastal Mountain Range and intersects Gorge Drive. Fifteen minutes after finishing breakfast, I parked the car in front of Theodore Martin's residence at 17000 Gorge Drive. It was a structure wrapped in dark brown shake siding with a lot of redwood and glass. The driveway from Gorge Drive dropped steeply to the courtyard area of the residence. The house sat on what looked to be an acre, thick with pine trees, and bordered on three sides by a redwood fence. A late-model, dark-colored series E Mercedes was parked in front of the three-car garage. I parked the car in the driveway near the front door and reviewed the instruction sheet one last time.

The doorbell was inaudible so I didn't know if it really rang. I waited a respectful fifteen seconds before pushing the button again. Five seconds later a thin, white male opened the door. He was about six-foot-two, and in his early forties. He looked like he had spent too much time in the sun for someone with a fair complexion. He needed a shave, and sunburned skin was peeling from his checks. I identified myself and told him why I was there. By the expression on his face, my explanation was immediately understood. At my request, he identified himself by showing me his driver's license. Theodore Allen Martin. Ted Martin had the wide-eyed look of a desperate man.

We shook hands, and he directed me to put the containers in the garage. He walked out into the courtyard to open the garage doors, making it clear that I was to unload the containers without his help. For some reason I didn't want him to think the containers were a strain for me to handle so I "macho'ed" them into the garage with nary a grunt. He wasn't impressed. With the containers secured in the garage, Martin signed the delivery receipt. We nodded good-bye and I was out of there. Mission completed. I felt relieved as I drove back down Page Mill Road. The job was essentially finished. No problems.

I knew the location of Dan Nelson's office building and twenty minutes later parked the big rented Oldsmobile in the lot behind the five-story building.

Nelson's office was a modest second-story three-room suite with several oriental rugs and enough dark mahogany to give the place the solid upper-class look. Through the glass walls separating the offices I could see a balcony that overlooked Castro Street, the main street in downtown Mountain View. The balcony sported enough greenery to replace the oxygen used by the daily people activities of the law firm. Two legal secretaries were hard at work when I walked into the office. My arrival caused the older of the two women to look up.

"May I help you?"

"I have an appointment with Mr. Nelson regarding a delivery from Florida."

At that comment, the younger of the two secretaries also looked up.

Nelson walked out of his office, arms open and a big smile on his face. He had an olive complexion, dark hair, and thought of himself as a lady-killer. In his younger days his slight edge of arrogance served as the proverbial hook on which the opposite sex regularly bit. My sister, Susan, had once taken the hook but never got reeled in. Well, I'd like to think.

"Harry! What a surprise. I thought you got out of the business for keeps when you left town. I heard you were making this delivery to Theodore Martin. What have you been up to? I talked to Susan about four months ago, and she didn't say anything about you leaving D.C. Why didn't you say good-bye when you left town? All of a sudden you were no longer available. And what about this boat of yours?"

Ignoring his questions I answered, "I was made an offer I couldn't refuse, and here I am. What kind of law are you practicing now?"

"I take most everything that comes through the door, and I stay pretty busy. What are you doing for lunch?"

His remark triggered the thought that I always considered Nelson to be an opportunist, and as such he wouldn't be able to specialize in any one area of law for fear of missing a good deal. I imagined him taking cases whether or not a case merited litigation. He would probably take the defense side of an intellectual property case knowing full well that his client actually stole the intellectual property. In answer to his question about lunch, I said, "I don't have much time. I'm flying back to Florida tonight at 8 p.m. from San Francisco and I thought I would drive over to Santa Cruz to see Susan."

"Say hello for me, O.K.? Listen, I need your help getting some information, and I wondered if I could count on you to give me a hand."

"I don't have much time to help you."

"Do you have to get right back? Can't you stay out here for a few days? I'll have my secretary change your flight schedule and I'll take care of any charges to make the change. What do you say?"

"Are you saying you want to hire me for a few days?"

"Well, yes, and I'll pay your going rate, whatever it is these days."

"I haven't had a going rate for a long time, but for you, it's sixty bucks an hour." I never had any qualms about taking money from attorneys, friends or otherwise. "And yes, I can reschedule my flight. I'm pretty flexible."

Nelson introduced me to his two member office staff, Bonnie and Gina. Bonnie cordially offered to take care of all the rescheduling arrangements for me. Gina kept typing through my introduction to her. I couldn't tell if she was totally absorbed in her work or just rude. Either way I really didn't care. I thanked Bonnie and mumbled a good-bye to Gina without getting a response.

I thought about the boat docked in Daytona Beach. I was working for the boat yard, in a way, so I felt sure it would be fine for another few days. I could use all the extra money I could get my hands on. I had no idea when I would be earning money again after getting back to the boat. I admit, I was a little charged being offered a PI assignment from an attorney after my two-year hiatus.

"Before we talk about me doing anything for you, I'm supposed to give you this signed receipt for the packages I delivered to Martin." I handed the receipt to Nelson who glanced at it as though it was unimportant, and stuffed it in his jacket pocket.

"What the hell was in those packages, and what's your connection to this delivery that was worth five-grand to some boat-yard bean counter in Daytona Beach?"

Nelson gave me a steady look, and said, "The packages contained heirlooms from an estate of a person whose son I represent in a probate case. The signed receipt was to insure that the record is kept straight. Martin got what was bequeathed to him in some old guy's will. Small world, okay Harry?"

I nodded in agreement, but was thinking that I just heard a lot of bull. I knew Nelson well enough to know that the steady, 'this is the truth,' look he gave me before answering my question regarding the packages was his inept manner of trying to make a lie sound like the truth. Nelson didn't owe me anything and whatever was going on with him and this package delivery was none of my business. Until or unless it did have something to do with me, why the hell should I care?

We left the office and walked north on Castro Street to a Chinese restaurant. After we ordered a couple of Chinese beers, some pot-stickers, and a large bowl of wor-won-ton soup, I got to the point of the lunch.

"What do you want me to do for you?" I was imagining some type of a surveillance assignment. Today, with the exception of most types of surveillance and person-to-person interviews, there aren't many things a PI can't do on-line. I was hoping that it was not a run-of-the-mill domestic surveillance. One marriage partner always wants to know what the other is up to, but can never adequately explain what he or she plans to do with the information. And worse, what the client may do to the other half once the results of the surveillance are in. More often than not the client gets angry at the PI for telling what the other half is up to. I got over it years ago. Nelson looked thoughtful and gave me the long steady look again. This time I dismissed the look knowing he would have no reason to lie to me regarding the reason for the assignment he was about to give me.

"Harry, my client is concerned that Theodore Martin may have already made arrangements to sell off the heirlooms for his own personal profit."

"So what if he does, they're his."

Nelson looked down for a moment and then looked up and said, "The will had a condition on the inheritance that the heirlooms must not be sold, but passed down to Martin's children. Martin and my client's father were good friends and I guess my client's father wanted to enrich Martin's family for generations to come. If Martin attempts to sell any of the heirlooms, my client is authorized by the will to recover them for his own family. Even though the will left my client substantial real estate holdings, he wants to have the heirlooms remain in his family."

"What's your client's name?" I asked casually.

"It's not important for the job I want you to do." Nelson said.

" Tell me what you want me to do, and I'll tell you if I think it's important." I was irritated at not being told all of the background.

"I want you to find where Martin spends his time and what he does. I want you to start right now and keep on him for the next two days, documenting all of his activity. Okay?"

After some quick mental gymnastics I said, "I'll do

the next two days and the remainder of today for twelve-hundred bucks. Here's my airline ticket. Have your secretary arrange a flight for me on Saturday. One other thing. I'll need to be paid in advance since I may not see you again before I leave. That all right with you?"

Nelson stared off into space for a few seconds and then, with a broad smile, nodded his agreement and took his checkbook from his jacket and wrote me a check for the twelve hundred. What a way to make a buck.

I didn't have a video or 35mm camera with me so the only information Nelson could get would be verbal. I did need to have a pair of binoculars. I was actually unprepared to take on the surveillance job, but I needed the bread.

When I was a working PI my duffel bag was always in the car. Over the years the duffel became full of the things I needed at one time or another, while on the job; binoculars, a 35mm camera with a 500 mm lens-attachment, a Sony 8mm video-camera, a tripod for the cameras, extra film for both cameras, a 9mm model 26 Glock pistol, pepper spray, two baseball caps, a change of shirts and underwear, a fake mustache, a hat with fake hair attached to its sides that made me look like a bum, a stun gun, and a radio-frequency scanner to know when the local fuzz had been notified by a nosy neighbor and dispatched to my location. I even carried a shaving kit with a small amount of everything that was usually in my medicine cabinet, including Rollaids, skin-cream, and sun-block. I still had most of the stuff, but the items were not together in the duffel bag. Being unprepared was not my style.

Nelson picked up the tab for the lunch and we walked back to his office where we parted ways. I went to my rented Olds and drove the two blocks to the bank on which Nelson's check was drawn. Getting back onto Castro

Street, I spotted a gun shop where I found a used (meaning beat-up) pair of 10 x 50 Bell & Howell binoculars for twenty-five bucks. I couldn't resist. I stopped at a convenience store on El Camino Real, and made a call to Martin's house to verify that he was at the residence. He answered the phone, and I hung up without saying anything. I picked up some snack food, a small bottle of water and a large bottle of water. The water in the large bottle would be thrown out and the bottle used to meet a greater need.

5

Page Mill Road is the only road connecting the valley floor to the homes on the mountain where Martin lived. It was 2:30 p.m. when I got to his house.

Gorge Drive is a two-lane asphalt road running from Page Mill Road to a dead-end in a canyon about a quarter of a mile past Martin's house. The shoulders of the road in front of his house were not wide enough to park a car. Even if they were, a car parked on the side of the road in this upscale neighborhood would attract too much attention. I drove back to Page Mill Road and parked uphill from Gorge Drive, in the shade of an old oak tree. I knew any passing county sheriff's patrol car would check me out, unconditionally, but nevertheless I sat slouched in the car so the local citizenry would not see me. I had my PI license with me and had dealt with the county cops many times. The drill goes like this.

"I'm a PI on a code 5," that's cop talk for a private sector surveillance, and they say, "Did you call it in," then I say, "The assignment came up suddenly, and I didn't have time, and my cell phone wasn't working, so I left it at the office." There's no substitute for experience.

After several hours of staring at the intersection where Martin's car would appear, I felt detached from my body. Totally alert, but only aware of my mind, and not my body. I was a pair of eyes that had became one with the car. To break the feeling, I searched for some fifties or sixties big-band music and found nothing but heavy rock and country-western. So much for the radio.

Being on surveillance is like playing hide-and-seek when I was a kid... excitement and heightened awareness. The excitement from the possibility of being burned by the subject, and the heightened awareness from paranoid feelings that anyone driving by knows exactly what I'm doing.

Martin's Mercedes appeared at the Page Mill Road intersection at 8:30 p.m. The moonlight was bright enough to silhouette the car and my twenty-five dollar binocs let in enough light to read his license tag with no problem.

I kept a one-curve distance between our cars going down the mountain, driving without headlights most of the time. When I got within a few blocks of normal city traffic I turned on my lights and began a normal tail. We continued on Page Mill Road to El Camino Real, the major north-south-business artery on the San Francisco peninsula. Martin turned south and drove through the corridor of fast food restaurants, motels, car washes, and strip malls to a dark storefront in Mountain View. The building was on the west side of the street and contained three storefronts facing El Camino Real.

    I parked a short distance north of the building and watched Martin park and walk to the front door of the middle store. In the light of an overhead sidewalk lamp, Martin appeared frazzled. His hair was disheveled, as though he had been vigorously massaging his scalp. His white T-shirt was spotted. His khaki pants looked tired, and he walked like he was upset and in a hurry.

    After Martin went into the middle store, I drove slowly past the building, which also housed a pizza joint and an adult bookstore. A small sign on Martin's front door, neatly lettered in gold leaf, read 'Project Management Success, Inc.' I parked a few yards north of the next intersection.

    Martin used a key to unlock the front door of Project Management Success. One minute went by before he came out of the store closing the front door behind him. He drove his car around the block, entered a narrow alley and parked in a small parking lot at the back of the store. There was no light at the back of the building. I parked across the alleyway in the parking lot of another building and watched him carry in the five containers I had delivered to him earlier that day. He struggled with the packages much more than I had. One strokes the ego whenever possible, but I reminded myself that he wasn't performing. The back door of the store stayed open while he carried in the containers. The light from a naked ceiling bulb illuminated, what appeared to be, an empty room. Martin closed the back door after carrying in the last bundle.

    I left the car and silently made my way to the back door. There was a small, high half window with no shades about five feet to the left of the door. The bottom of the window was level with the top of the door. I looked around for something to stand on. If I hadn't already met Martin I would have stumbled into the back room under some sort of pretext, like thinking it was part of the adult video store next door. The pizza store had a stack of boxes beside its back door that happened to be supporting a six-foot A-frame ladder. Just as I started to spread the ladder under the window, the back door of the porn shop opened outward, flooding the area with light. I quickly leaned the ladder against the wall, turned my back and started fiddling with the zipper on my fly.

I could hear Martin moving things inside the back room. The guy who came out of the porn shop walked across the alley to his car paying me no attention. The porn shop door closed of its own accord. After the lights of the porn customer's car had disappeared I positioned the ladder and climbed up to take a look.

I could see the entire room. There were two gray metal boxes placed against the wall that separated the front and back rooms. One device was the size of a small top-loading freezer and the other the size of a two-drawer filing cabinet. There were a variety of computer-type lights on the front of the large box and no lights on the smaller box. Large diameter electric cords ran from each box to a 220-volt outlet on the wall separating the room from the porn shop. The door connecting the back room with the front of the store was on my right adjacent to the pizza joint wall.

Martin opened one of the delivered containers and pulled out a one-inch thickness of some kind of paper. The paper sheets were the same size as the package they came out of. He carried the paper with both hands and placed it vertically into a wide slot at the end of the larger of the two machines. He took an aluminum-framed sheet of paper from his brief case, which was sitting on top of the large machine. The paper in the frame looked like a sheet of eight-and-a-half by eleven white computer-printer paper. A crisp looking U.S. greenback bill occupied the center of the paper. Like someone threw cold water on me, it shockingly dawned on me that I was witnessing the printing of counterfeit money. I had a fleeting sensation that possibly my senses were beginning to dull, I mean, the shape of the containers, watching Martin pull sheets of paper from a box to put into the machine... family jewels my ass. I was suddenly never more alert. I couldn't make out the numbers but could tell there was a two-digit number on the bill. When Martin placed the aluminum frame vertically into a slot at the top of the small machine, I could see that the bill was exposed on both sides of the frame.

    Martin manipulated a few switches and pushed a button. Some of the lights on the larger machine blinked. A muted humming noise came through the window glass. Paper slowly began coming out of the larger of the two machines, automatically stacking itself on a tray extending from the end of the machine. A copy job. But one Kinko's couldn't handle. The sheets of paper coming out of the machine were uncut sheets of currency just like those that come off the presses at the U.S. Treasury Department's printing operations in D.C. and Fort Worth.

    I remembered reading that the new twenty, fifty, and one hundred-dollar bills were being made with paper loaded with anti-counterfeit technology. The article had mentioned there being only one company in the U.S. that could produce this paper, and, of course, the company had the exclusive contract with the federal government.

    I quickly went back to my car and grabbed the binoculars. The money was still coming out when I got back to the window. I could see that the bills were twenties.

There were eight rows and four columns of twenties on each sheet. I estimated there to be one thousand sheets of paper in each of the five containers. Martin was going to print one hundred and sixty thousand twenty-dollar bills or three million two hundred thousand bucks.

California PI license holders are required by law to report the occurrence of any known felony. Not that I stick strictly to the rules, but I had to do something, I couldn't just know about it and walk away. I knew then that I would be contacting the local PD or Sheriff's Office to report this crime. I just didn't know when, yet. I continued watching. The sheets of money were coming out of the machine at the rate of one every thirty seconds. I stayed fifteen minutes and witnessed the production of nineteen thousand two hundred dollars. What a business. At this rate Martin could print a little more than six hundred and fourteen thousand dollars in eight non-stop hours. It would take him about forty-two hours to print all the sheets I had delivered to him.

After watching for fifty minutes I went back to my car. According to the unwritten law of the surveillance operative, I would have to stay with Martin as long as he was out and about. Less professional PI's would more than likely call it quits at this point, and there would be those who would be devising a plan to grab a bunch of the funny money for their own gain, but that's not the face I want to see in the mirror each morning. The wait was long and the night was getting colder. I didn't want to start the car to run the heater for fear of being discovered in a back-alley parking lot behind a porn shop in the middle of the night. Martin had arrived at the store at about 9:00 p.m. and it was 2:00 a.m. when the lights went off in the back room. Martin walked out of the back door empty-handed and locked the door behind him. If the local black-bag boys only knew.

    I followed Martin back to his house and waited an appropriate amount of time before leaving my surveillance spot on Page Mill Road to drive by his house. It was now 3:00 a.m. and the house was totally dark. Since Martin had not returned to the Page Mill Road intersection and his car was not in sight, I was confident that he had put his car in the garage and gone to bed. I headed back to the motel to get a few hours sleep before going to see Nelson in the morning.

6

I woke unassisted, grabbed a quick shave, some clean clothes, and was out the door. Driving to Nelson's place I passed Martin's 'PMS' storefront and visualized the moneymaking machines waiting to pump out the bogus twenties.

Nearing Nelson's office, I focused on the identification of his client. Given the present circumstances I was sure he would level with me. I didn't think Nelson would knowingly involve himself in such a serious criminal act. It didn't appear as though he was in major need of money, and my long but intermittent association with him didn't clue me into him being a closet criminal. One thing I did know was that I had been used to commit a felony. I was a little pissed for having been taken advantage of so easily. At times, I lie to myself to protect the ego. Who was

I kidding? I knew from the start that things weren't on the up-and-up with this delivery gig. Greed has been the root of many of my mistakes. A truth I had long recognized.

I got to Nelson's office at 9:15 a.m. I could see through the open door into his private office. He was talking to Bonnie. She looked to be about sixty, and was trim and neatly dressed. Her short gray hair, olive complexion and casual sport clothes gave her an air of warmth and gentle confidence. It was clear that she was the force behind the office management.

Gina was a striking contrast to Bonnie and I wondered when, and under what circumstances, she had been hired. She was in her late twenties and was wearing jeans, brown boots, and a skin-tight blouse that made it easy to count her rolls of fat. Her hair was the texture of orange-brown straw and her black lipstick and two-inch nails didn't improve the image. She was talking on the phone in a manner that left no doubt that it was a personal call. I overheard her say, "I'm not going to spend the night with that bastard after what he did on our last ride."

I noticed a small red tattoo of a shield containing the number eighty-one on the front of her upper left arm. Non-member supporters of the Hells Angels use the red shield and the number eighty-one as an icon. The eight for the eighth letter and the one for the first letter in the alphabet. Gina was, or used to be, a biker's "old lady." I couldn't accuse Nelson of discrimination in hiring.

Nelson saw me in the outer office and abruptly cut off his conversation with Bonnie. Bonnie came out of the office. She nodded recognition of my presence and extended her arm in a gesture that said for me to go in. Nelson was sitting on the front edge of his desk, nattily dressed, and looking tired.

"What did you find?" He asked in a matter of fact tone of voice.

I looked directly at him trying to detect any body movements that indicated stress or deception, like eyes cast downward, fingers to the nose or mouth area, shaking of one foot, sudden perspiration on the face, and things like that. "Oh not much, just that the packages I delivered to Martin contained U.S. currency paper, not objects of art, and Martin is in the process of printing several million bucks in counterfeit twenties, and I'm guilty of aiding and abetting that criminal act."

Nelson's eyes widened in an expression that I interpreted to be his interpretation of a surprised appearance. Being suspicious and cynical, I was probably reading meaning into an otherwise innocent reaction, but my impression didn't change.

"What? Did you actually see him printing money?"

"You bet your ass I did. I watched him print nineteen thousand bucks and then waited out of sight while he printed another three hundred and forty five thousand, making a grand total of about three hundred sixty five thousand for the night, which, by the way, ended at 3:00 a.m. What's going on here?"

"I have no idea, I can only tell you what I know, and that's what my client told me."

"You're wearing me out Nelson, who is the client?"

"I'm not able to tell you that."

"That's nonsense. We're dealing with a major federal crime here. I'm involved, and I want some answers." I was getting hot.

"I don't have any answers, other than what I've already told you. I'm representing a client whose father died and left this bunch of stuff to Theodore Martin. My client wants to make sure the stuff stays with Martin or else gets returned to him according to the old man's will." Nelson's voice was almost pleading, and it made him believable. He added, "Right now I want you to take me to where you saw Martin printing money."

Nelson was my client, even though our relationship didn't resemble anything I'd previously experienced with other clients. Whatever information I developed regarding the assignment he had given me was rightfully his. I wished I had held back the information about the money printing until I determined the ID of his client. I knew I would be bringing the Secret Service into the picture, but I wanted to follow the drama a little longer before taking that step. I wasn't ready to be told to back off and mind my own business, like a good little citizen. The ego monster was alive.

I agreed to take Nelson to the money-printing site. We left his office amidst stares from the two secretaries. Half-way out the door, Nelson turned to the two women and said that he'd be back in an hour.

I tried to get Nelson to voluntarily give me the whole story while we drove the short distance to PMS, Inc. Just before reaching the store I said in a solemn voice, "You know Nelson, you're as guilty as I am on this thing. If I were you I'd tell me everything I know and let me check it out. Hell, you've already paid me for the time and your ass is on the line for this thing if the news gets out."

"Okay, okay, I get it. I'm telling you I can't let you know anything until I talk with my client. I know I have exposure here and I'll deal with it, but I need to talk with my client first, understand?"

Nelson looked straight ahead while talking to me. I drove into the parking area behind the group of three stores, parking directly behind PMS, Inc. Martin's car was not parked in front, or in back of the store. We got out of the car. Nelson stood by the car door, and I started to go for the ladder by the pizza joint when I noticed the door to Martin's store was not completely closed. I walked up to the door, and found splintered wood around the lock, and on the step leading up to the door. "Come on, I've got a feeling we're not going to see anything."

The room was bare. Striped of machines, paper and power cables.

"This room had a scanning machine and a printing machine in here last night. Martin went home at 2:00 a.m. and he left the machines, the unused paper and the printed money in this store. What do you know about this guy Martin?"

Nelson's eyes were opened wide and with a moment's hesitation, he replied, "I didn't have him checked out, if that's what you mean. Didn't have any reason to. He told me he was a research scientist at SRI in Menlo Park and that's all I know."

Stanford Research Institute, like MIT, Cal Tech, and Bell Labs is a major player in many state-of-the-art technologies. The one area of work I had once heard a spokesman from SRI comment on was artificial intelligence. At the time, they were using it applied to speech recognition. However, the spokesman had stated that AI projects were also underway in the disciplines of imaging and graphics.

"Do you know what kind of research he is involved in?" Nelson looked like he was in deep thought. It took a few seconds for my question to register. Then he said, "Yeah, he's a xerography expert, you know, he works on projects involving super-advanced methods for copying paper images."

"Sounds right to me. Looks like he may have developed himself a little printing press."

Nelson gave a nod and said that he had to go back to his office. As we walked out the back door Nelson said,

"Drop me off and then wait at your hotel for me to call you around noon. Okay Harry?"

I said okay, and immediately decided to drive to Martin's house after dropping Nelson. I wanted to get some answers. Nelson didn't want to give any. I felt a self-imposed pressure to quickly gain an understanding of how the counterfeiting operation was put together. I needed to inform the Secret Service of the counterfeit operation in a timely manner to prevent them from accusing me of withholding evidence in a federal crime. The trickel down of that action would cause the California bureaucracy to revoke my PI license.

7

When I turned onto Gorge drive from Page Mill Road, I could see the flashing lights of a Sheriff's patrol car at the entrance to Martin's driveway. Even though it was well before noon, the early morning fog had not yet totally burned off and the lights were out of focus. My pulse quickened when I saw yellow crime-scene tape stretched across the entrance to the property. The Sheriff's car was being used to further block any attempts to enter. I parked partially on the road and partially on the shoulder about twenty yards short of the driveway. There were three other cars parked in the area at the foot of the driveway. One vehicle was a cargo van with a crime-scene investigation sign below the Sheriff's Department logo. I walked to the tape, ducked under and proceeded down the driveway when an officer appeared from the front door.

"Hold it right there sir." The officer said, holding up one arm, his hand pushing against the air. I stopped and he walked up the driveway to my position.

"What's going on?" I said.

"May I please see some identification sir?" the officer said, in a way that left no doubt that he was in control here.

I pulled out my wallet and offered my driver's license. My PI license was visible in the opposing plastic insert. "I came to see if I could get a copy of a receipt for a delivery I made to Mr. Martin yesterday."

"So, you're a PI?"

"Yeah, what's going on?"

"Mr. Martin is dead. Shot in the head, maybe by an intruder. Can't tell yet. The cleaning woman found him when she got to work this morning about nine.

The deputy affected a stance that told me that he felt important telling me the news. A talkative cop. Probably has an unrewarding future with the department.

"The detectives are in there trying to figure it out right now. Wait right here, they may want to talk to you."

In about two minutes the officer appeared at the front door motioning me to come into the house. A Santa Clara County Sheriff's detective greeted me when I entered the large living room. He introduced himself as Detective Clark. Clark was a short, dark, overweight, middle-aged man who looked like he had indigestion. He needed a shave. His suit needed pressing.

"I understand from Officer Chandler that you had some dealings with the deceased yesterday, something about a delivery. What was it that you delivered to him?"

"If the deceased is Theodore Martin, I delivered five containers to him yesterday morning around 9:30 a.m."

"That's who it is all right, what was in the containers?"

"I didn't open them but my client in Daytona Beach, Florida, told me the containers contained art objects and jewelry."

"I don't see any containers lying around here anywhere. How big were they?" I described the size and weight of the containers and related the story about losing the receipt and coming up here now to ask Martin to sign another receipt. I held back any further information. The detective made notes of what I had said and then asked for my name, address, and telephone number in case they needed to contact me. I told him that I was due to leave town permanently on the following day. Clark told me I should alter my plans until he told me it was okay to leave. I nodded agreement and asked, "Does it look like a suicide?" I asked, to check the information the deputy gave me on my way in.

Avoiding the question, Clark offered his opinion that Martin had been dead for several hours and by way of dismissing me he said, "The coroner has to check it out and he'll let us know. Thank you for your cooperation Mr. Caine."

I left the house, walked up to my car and sat thinking for a few minutes. I had not seen a body. It had either been removed or was possibly in another part of the house. Since I hadn't seen the forensic guys or a police photographer, it was a good bet that the body was in another part of the house, like a bedroom. Assuming the killer is the person who took the machines, paper and printed money, he or they would want to complete the theft and murder under the cloak of darkness. That meant

Martin would have been shot sometime between 3:00 a.m. and 6:00 a.m. My theory was that the bad guy or guys came to Martin's house, probably got him out of bed, got him to tell them or take them to where the machines and money were. They wouldn't have shot him until they had the machines and paper, and they would have had plenty of time to get to the store and empty it out before anyone came around. The neighboring stores probably didn't open before 9:00 a.m.

I got back to the motel at 11:05 a.m. and walked across the street for breakfast. While eating sunny-side up eggs, hash browns, bacon, and a couple of pancakes, I mentally reviewed the names and connections I could make with people I knew to be involved with the money paper.

Zucker directed me to deliver it to Martin and to give the receipt to Nelson. Scarapelli Express, of Fernadina Beach Florida, brought the paper to the airport. What I needed to know was where the paper came from and how Zucker knew Martin and Nelson.

I went back to the motel to wait for Nelson's call and used the wait-time to contact an information provider.

Ten years ago, information was obtained via phone calls and pavement pounding. Today, there was immediate user-friendly access to billions of on-line records on the Internet. For those reactionaries who never got with the dot-com program there is the fax machine, and the telephone. I'm Internet literate, but I hadn't used any on-line information for over two years, and didn't remember the website addresses, passwords, or user ID's. But, I did have an old list of telephone numbers, and account numbers for a few vendors, hidden in the recesses of my wallet.

I called an info-vendor that I still had an open account with, even though two and a half years had gone since I last used their services. After satisfying them that I was who I said I was, I was provided with their website address along with my ID and password into their system. They verified that the credit card number they had for me was still valid and immediately took my request for a name search on Martin, Nelson, and Zucker.

After ten minutes of waiting in my room while I watched the local TV news, weather and sports, Nelson called, asking me to meet him in his office at 2:00 p.m.

I agreed to meet him and quickly added, "Theodore Martin was shot and killed at his home early this morning." I said it in a way that tacitly asked what the hell had I gotten myself into?

After five seconds of silence, Nelson said in a dead serious and slightly overly dramatic voice, "We need to talk, Harry. Come over here right now."

"I'll be there in about fifteen minutes."

On the way out of the motel, I found I had received replies to my three name searches. I had a hit on all three.

A hit on a name search gets you a social security number, the reported current and previous addresses on file for the subject along with the time frames in which they were reported. Also reported are any other social security number(s) the subject used, listed telephone numbers if available, and known AKA's.

Using the social security numbers I got from the name searches, I faxed a request for three 'personal profiles'.

The 'personal profile' request required that I supply a subject's social security number, and in return for that little goodie I could determine a bunch of things, including an address history, corporations in which the subject is an officer, bankruptcy filings, business loans guaranteed by physical collateral, and relatives of the subject.

I folded the name search results and stuffed them into my shirt pocket for later review of the addresses. I promised myself I'd find an Internet cafe, or a library, or somewhere that I could go on-line the next time I needed information. A person's address history can tell an interesting story.

Bonnie was typing and looked up at me with a worried look as I entered Nelson's office. Gina was wearing earphones and continued typing without looking up. Bonnie motioned me to go into Nelson's office, and I walked in closing the door behind me. Nelson stood up in back of his desk, and with upturned palms and a wrinkled brow said, "Look Harry, I didn't know things would get like this. I didn't think anyone would be killed."

I listened and framed a few questions while he spoke. "Start from the beginning. How did Zucker get connected with Martin?"

"I met Martin at a cocktail party about a year ago. He told me he was a researcher at SRI and that he had been moonlighting on his own project, which was almost finished. He was developing a prototype device that can copy any document in such detail that it's impossible to tell the copy from the original. It's like cloning the original object as long as the medium of the copy is the same as the original. He asked me if I had ever done any patent work. I told him I had, and he made an appointment to discuss my handling the patent process for him. He showed up at my office, had me sign a non-disclosure agreement, and then gave me the drawings and written descriptions of the copy machine he had developed. Put the whole thing in my hands. Gave me a check for two-thousand and said if that was not enough he would give me more at our next meeting." Nelson had thrown this information out as though he was trying to get rid of it. He paused for a moment and I said, "Okay, Nelson. Relax. Tell me who you introduced him to, and who asked you to do it."

Nelson's reply was delayed a few seconds and the thought occurred to me that he was using the time to make up the next lie. I glanced through the glass dividers separating the office from the support staff. Both women were typing and Gina was still wearing earphones as she typed. The advances in personal computing had obviously not reduced the amount of typing required to produce the paper needed to run a law office.

"Zucker and I were friends when we were students at Harvard. We've occasionally been in touch since that time. About a year ago, Zucker asked me what was new in the high-tech world of California and I told him in general about the gadget Martin had invented without disclosing any detail. After all, I signed a non-disclosure agreement, which I was not going to violate. It was just idle conversation. I never thought anymore about it until I got a call from Zucker last month. He told me that he was planning on shipping a few packages to my client, Martin, and asked me to receive the receipt of the delivery of the packages. He also told me that if anyone asked, the packages contained small pieces of art from the probate estate of one of my clients."

"How did Zucker know how to contact Martin?" I asked.

"I told him Martin was a research scientist for SRI, and I guess he took it from there."

"So you really didn't know what was in the packages?"

"Not a clue. I was just doing Zucker a favor. I called Martin after talking to Zucker just to touch base. I thought he would tell me if Zucker contacted him, but he didn't say a word about it. I didn't want to mention it if he didn't bring it up."

"Didn't you ask Zucker why he contacted Martin? After all, Zucker only knew of Martin from the fact that you were handling the paperwork for the patent on Martin's invention."

"Yeah, I asked him, and he said that Martin's work interested him and that he had a business proposition he thought Martin would be interested in. I offered to be an intermediary for Zucker, but he refused the offer saying that it was a simple matter that he could handle himself. I let it drop and the next thing I know, you're delivering the receipt of the packages to me. I had no idea what Martin and Zucker were involved in. Now that I know Martin was involved in printing bogus money, I can think of many reasons why someone would want to kill him."

My gut told me Nelson was either lying or leaving out a lot of relevant information.

"Are you willing to foot my expenses for a few extra days while I make some inquires about Martin?"

Nelson looked pained at my question. "This is not our business, Harry. Let the police handle it. Your best bet would be to go back to your boat and forget about all this."

"I can't do that. I've been requested by the Sheriff's Department to stick around. They may want to talk to me. They know I'm a licensed PI, and they expect me to cooperate. I want to cooperate. We're both involved in this thing, and you know as well as I that his death is connected to the money printing."

Nelson looked pale, as though he was in shock. He was rubbing his chin, the side of his nose, and running his fingers through his hair. Perspiration was beading on his forehead and upper lip.

"All right, Harry. You poke around, I'll pay your expenses plus an additional five hundred for two additional days providing you let me know everything you find. And I don't need to remind you that any information you develop belongs to me. That'll make seventeen hundred for four and a half days work. Right, Harry? Is it a deal?"

"You got a deal. I'll be in touch."

To close the conversation, Nelson said, "I'll have Bonnie make your return reservation to Daytona Beach so that you leave Sunday evening. Okay?"

Now I felt that Nelson wanted me to get the hell out of his hair ASAP. I said, "Hold off on that, I need the Sheriff's permission to leave town. I'll tell Bonnie later when to make my return reservation."

Nelson nodded agreement and wrote a five hundred dollar check made out to me and handed it over. I figured Nelson wanted to find a way to protect himself from any future liability, and it was worth it to him to let me investigate. We shook hands. I walked out of the office and went straight to his bank.

8

After stopping at the bank to cash the check, I went back to the motel. Three multi-page faxes were waiting for me. The volume of paper appeared to bother the superior-acting desk clerk. Tough.

Back in my room, I spread the documents on my bed in Martin, Zucker, and Nelson piles. I compared the previous addresses, corporate connections, fictitious business name filings and Universal Commercial Code listings, hoping to spot a connection among them. Nelson and Zucker were listed as residing in Boston during the same time period. This vaguely confirmed Nelson's claim to have met Zucker while both were students at Harvard. Martin's history and business connections didn't intersect with Zucker's or Nelson's.

It was almost 1:00 p.m. when I drove back to Nelson's office in hopes of finding Bonnie alone. I did. As I entered the office, Bonnie informed me that Nelson would be back around two o'clock. I assumed Gina's absence was due to the lunch break. I said, "You're aware of what happened to Mr. Martin and that I've been retained by Nelson?" Bonnie nodded affirmative and I asked, "Can you tell me anything about Theodore Martin?"

Bonnie looked toward the ceiling for a moment, and then said, "He has only been in the office once that I know of, and I only met him briefly during that one time. He looked like my idea of a scientist. You know, disheveled hair, wrinkled clothes, and shoes that looked like he had been dragged across sand paper, by the arms."

"Was a background check run on Martin?"

I didn't think I would get a yes to that one and was surprised when Bonnie said, "We didn't run any kind of a check on him from the office, but Dan hired an outside guy. I think the guy is a PI. I'm surprised Dan didn't tell you about that."

So was I. I would have conducted a background check on Martin had the assignment been oriented toward an invesigation instead of a delivery. "What's the guy's name?"

Bonnie thought for a moment and said, "I never met him but there were several calls from him and a letter which I assumed was a report of his investigation. I never read the letter or saw an invoice, but I recall the name on the return address. It was Max Kincaid. I thought the name stood out, you know, different."

"Thanks for your help, Bonnie. By the way, where's Gina Today?"

"She's on a 'run' with her boyfriend. She's into motorcycles and all that. She'll be in the office tomorrow."

"Maybe I'll catch her later."

I left the office and headed for the first public telephone. I found it at the corner bookstore. I dialed the information operator and asked if there was a listing in the Bay area for Max Kincaid. Kincaid's number was provided in addition to a Mountain View address. I drove to the address, which was four blocks south of PMS, Inc.

I parked the car and walked across the driveway to the door of an office whose sign read 'Kincaid Research'. I opened the door and looked into a very small outer office containing a secretary's desk and a filing cabinet. Both had seen better days. The room was empty. I called in a loud voice. "Mr. Kincaid?"

I could hear adhesive tape being pulled from its roll in the office behind a closed door at the back of the secretary's office. The door opened and a man of medium height, in his early forties, balding, slightly overweight, and needing a shave walked into the secretarial area. He wore baggy jeans, a white sweatshirt spotted with food, and untied, dirty-white sneakers. The office had a musty smell, and the man who walked in looked like he belonged. He had a surprised look that told me he didn't get frequent walk-in traffic. The man asked, "Can I help you?"

"Are you Max Kincaid?"

"That's me."

"My name's Harry Caine. I'm a PI. Your name came up regarding an investigation I'm conducting. I was wondering if you could share some information with me. Are you a licensed PI?"

"I used to be. Now I just do research, if you know what I mean."

I knew what he meant all right. He probably ran his professional life as sloppily as he appeared and ultimately

53

had his license pulled for some unethical, immoral, or illegal behavior. He was operating as a PI, without a license. A definite no-no in California.

"I was hoping for a little professional courtesy." I said, trying to make him feel as though he belonged to the club.

"Professional courtesy doesn't pay the rent, hotshot. If you want something I have, it's gonna cost you. You think I get the stuff for free?"

I was dealing with an asshole and the only way to deal with one is to be one. Using my tough voice I said, "I hear you did some 'research' on a guy by the name of Theodore Martin. Is that right?"

"Yeah, I watched the geek for a while. You want to know what I saw?"

"You're quick."

"I busted my ass to get the info I got on Martin and I wasn't particularly well paid for it. You know how cheap attorneys are."

Letting the generalization hang in the air, I fished out a fifty-dollar bill and replied, "Will this help?"

"Now I feel more like sharing."

"Wonderful, tell me what you have on Martin."

"Where did you hear that I had information on Martin?"

"From a confidential source. Isn't the fifty enough?"

Kincaid fidgeted with a piece of paper and momentarily looked at the floor before looking me in the eyes and saying, "Okay Caine. As a professional courtesy. And I want you to know that I don't make it a habit of divulging information that a client has paid for. You know, it ain't ethical."

This was an irritating guy, and, unfortunately, in this business you don't have to look far to find guys like him.

That thought triggered an unpleasant feeling that I would be living on the moral fringe, just like Kincaid, for withholding knowledge of the conterefeit operation. Life consists of the circumstances that make you act the way you do. "Skip the fiction. Just tell me what you found." I wondered where in the hell Nelson found this guy, but I wondered less aggressively.

Kincaid looked pleased when he said, "I know you're working for Dan Nelson, the cheap bastard."

Kincaid's eyes widened and his eyebrows arched, which I interpreted to mean something like 'Do you know what I mean'. He looked as though he was enjoying the role of being asked for information from another PI. Kincaid sat down in the secretary's chair, leaned back and put his feet on the desk.

"According to the divorce file, Martin was married for about fifteen years before his wife got a belly full of his fourteen hour-a-day, seven-day-a-week work schedule. The divorce happened four years ago. The ex got half of everything. Her take was one and a half million. He kept the house, car, the debts, and was ordered by the court to pay her two grand a month for life until she decides to remarry. She took half of his 401K and half of his stock portfolio. He has no criminal record and no bankruptcies. In my report, I said he was strapped for cash and probably for sex because he went to a porn-shop down the street every night."

Kincaid gestured with his arm pointing to El Camino in the direction of Palo Alto. He continued.

"After Nelson read my report, he asked if I could document Martin visiting the porn-shop. I asked him if he wanted video of Martin going into the shop and he told me to video his activity inside the shop as well. I had to buy some body-worn video equipment and it cost me a bundle. Anyway, I video'd the genius inside the porn shop while he was in one of the private booths. The wall between the booth he was in and the adjoining booth I was in was a piece of translucent plastic. You can push a button in the booth and the wall will go clear if the person in the adjoining booth has also pushed the clear button. They call them 'buddy booths'. Christ! I stood in my booth, pushed the button and there was Martin on his knees at the fly of some young stud. I was wearing a wristwatch camera with a mini-VCR recorder in a fanny-pack. I recorded the whole thing. I acted like a pervert who gets his kicks out of watching. I turned the tape over to Nelson. He paid me and that was the last I heard of it. That was about six months ago. Martin into some kind of trouble?"

"A little", I said. "Someone shot and killed him this morning."

Kincaid's eyes widened, "You didn't hear nothing from me, Caine. You got that?"

"Yeah, I got that, Kincaid. Try to keep out of trouble." I walked out of the door.

It was a no-brainer that Nelson used the video to blackmail Martin into printing money with his new invention. Martin may have figured he couldn't afford to have his porn-shop activities become public. SRI wouldn't take kindly to the news. It was not easy to see Nelson as a blackmailer and counterfeiter, but facts are facts. Until I could prove otherwise, Nelson was a blackmailer.

Back at the motel, I called Susan at her house in Santa Cruz. She has always been a cheerleader for me and I've always been proud of her accomplishments and of her character. She seemed to know the right thing to do in most circumstances, and as far as I could tell, she always did the right thing. Nelson had been infatuated with her from the time he first met her during our junior year in college. They had dated until he went away to Harvard. I lost track of their relationship after that.

We brought each other up to date before I asked, "Are you and Dan Nelson still seeing each other?"

Without hesitation she replied, "He calls once or twice a year and that's about all. The last time I talked with him was about three months ago. He called to say hello and ask how I was doing. Why? What's going on Harry? Are you working on a case? How do you come back in town for a day or so and get an assignment?"

Susan's questions were rapid fire and although I could answer all of them I thought it best to let them hang. I wasn't sure what Nelson was up to, but my gut told me not to involve her any more than was necessary. In a casual manner I said, "Yeah I'm doing a small investigation, nothing important, mainly I just wanted to say hello. How about I pop over the hill this evening for dinner with you?"

Susan hesitated a moment. "Okay. What time?"

"I'll be over around 7:00. Okay?"

"Okay. We'll go to the Crow's Roost." Susan sounded excited and happy.

The Crow's Roost was a popular Santa Cruz waterfront restaurant and I agreed to meet her there.

It was 3:30 p.m. when I got off the phone with Susan. It would take me one hour to drive to Santa Cruz, leaving me two and a half hours to try and find a few answers.

9

Aside from the identity of Martin's murderer, I wanted to know how and where Zucker got the currency paper. Was Martin's killer tied to the source of the paper? Was Nelson involved in Martin's murder, or was the murder just a random act? It had been a long time since I had a real investigation to work on, and I was excited. It was the same feeling I used to get when I first started in the business. Technically, I wasn't hired to investigate the murder, but I wasn't going to just let it go. Since I owed Nelson an investigative effort through Sunday, I would apply myself.

The only connection I had to the paper was Zucker and the name of the delivery company that brought the paper to the Daytona Beach airport.

Back at the hotel I called my friendly info-vendor requesting a corporate profile on Scarapelli Express of Jacksonville. The return would be faxed, as a matter of company policy, and would have the names of the officers or owners of the company, as well as any loans, liens, or judgments, which can lead to other revealing information about the lives of those involved. I called the front desk, and asked them to call my room when the fax arrived. The fax would have no meaning to the desk clerk. It's not the most secure way to operate, but, lacking my own private fax machine, it was a chance I needed to take.

I used the response wait time to decide on the attitude I would assume the next time I talked to Nelson. I was more than a little pissed at him, but then he didn't select me to do the courier job, and I imagined that he was having just as much trouble trying to figure out what to tell me when we next talked. I didn't believe Nelson had it in him to kill someone, or to have a person killed. He would have to be death-defyingly desperate, and I didn't detect that during our conversations over the past twenty-four hours. It was likely that he had stumbled into this thing with Martin, and it became a target of opportunity. Would Nelson use blackmail just because the opportunity presented itself? He may have believed he could carry off the blackmail and the delivery of the money to Zucker without being detected. He could have forced Martin to produce the counterfeit twenties in the Bay Area and, as planned, ship the loot back to a distribution point somewhere on the East Coast. Nelson was likely going to get his cut of the deal from Zucker after the bogus money was received back east.

The Scarapelli Express information arrived twenty-five minutes later. When the desk clerk called my room, he informed me that the hotel was installing an internet

59

computer in the lobby, and that it would be available tomorrow morning. Small things make life easier.

The fax indicated that Scarapelli Express was a subsidiary of Florida Coast Paper, Inc., a company that had been in business for five years in Fernandina Beach, Florida. The profile stated that the CEO and Chairman of the Board for Florida Coast Paper was Anthony Falcon. The information further indicated that Falcon was previously the Operations Officer for the ENARC Company in Massachusetts, and prior to that, the Operations Officer for Zucker Industries, a trash hauling company with headquarters in Patterson, New Jersey. I felt an electric tingle in my stomach, which is the signal from my brain to the lower forty that I have just received very significant information. I recalled a magazine article about ENARC The article told how ENARC had been the sole supplier of U.S. currency paper since the mid-eighteen hundreds. That they use cotton fibers to make the paper, mainly scraps from clothing manufacturing firms, and that a large amount of their raw material comes from recycled blue jeans. The article also talked about the 'security thread' ENARC developed and had integrated into the currency paper for the purpose of putting counterfeiters out of business.

I faxed a request for a New Jersey Secretary of State corporate record check on Zucker Industries. The reply listed Moshe Zucker, Sr. as the CEO and Chairman of the Board. Now the hair was standing up on the back of my neck. This was like discovering a fishing hole where each cast of the line brought in a big one.

I called Zucker in Daytona Beach. Burkholder answered the phone and informed me that Zucker had been waiting to hear from me. In a seductive tone she said,

"Don't go away Sweetie, he'll be right with you." It appeared that Burkholder had taken our relationship to a new level. A shiver went through me from top to bottom. I hoped there was a way I could get my boat out of the boat yard without going up to Zucker's office.

Zucker came on the line in a high-pitched voice, "Caine! It's about time you let me know what the hell's going on. Did the delivery go all right?

I decided to play it like I knew the story and let Zucker try to deny it.

"I guess you think I'm stupid, Zucker. Do you really think I believed your family jewels story? Yeah, Martin got the paper and now Martin is dead. Shot this morning. Martin's counterfeiting machines and the currency paper are gone, along with a bunch of 'new' money. That shouldn't bother you though. You're probably responsible. And even if you lose the paper you can always get more from ENARC through you friends at Florida Coast Paper."

I left it there for what felt like ten seconds of awkward silence. When he spoke again his voice was calm and tentative.

"What the hell are you talking about, Caine?"

It was a feeble attempt at innocence and to stick it to him again I said, "I'm talking about your buddy Falcon. What's he, Zucker, a family connection from when he worked for your old man in New Jersey? Or does he still work for your old man? You guys have probably been waiting a long time to use Falcon to supply the paper for printing bogus money, and then Nelson handed you Theodore Martin."

Zucker hesitated and then in an angry voice said, "I don't know what you're trying to do, Caine, but I'll tell you one thing, keep your nose out of other people's business or you won't have a boat waiting for you to pick up. Did I ask you to play detective out there? I don't know about any shooting or any counterfeiting operation. Just do what you were paid for and get back here and take your boat the hell out of this boat yard. Damn! Is that clear, Caine?"

I heard the receiver slam down. Sometimes I get carried away. With the Sheriff's permission, I could get the hell out of Dodge and go get my boat, or I could poke around here a little longer. Poking around was my favorite thing and anyway there was no way I could get a plane reservation changed before tomorrow. Also, I owed Nelson a couple of days of investigation, and I didn't need to let Zucker know what I was doing. Zucker left the return flight open so I could return at my liesure and that's how I'll play it.

I sat a while longer in my hotel room considering Nelson's connection with Zucker and the counterfeiting operation. No answers. Lots of possibilities, most of which put Nelson in a very bad light and quite possibly in harms way.

10

I didn't think Susan would be able to shed any light on Nelson's activities, but that was a secondary reason for the visit. I was looking forward to seeing her. A good fish dinner would be a bonus. I left the hotel at six and made my way across the Oregon Expressway to U.S. 101 then south on Highway 17 over the Santa Cruz Mountains. The drive across Highway 17 is like being on a curvy, hilly, slot-car track with the evening commuter traffic moving at sixty miles an hour. By the time I got to Santa Cruz, I needed a massage to get my hands pried off the steering wheel. Highway 17 ends by merging into Ocean Street in Santa Cruz. Passing the Santa Cruz County Civic Center brought back memories of the many trips to that concrete structure to research properties and view criminal records. It had been about four years since I had been in Santa Cruz, and it appeared that nothing had changed.

I arrived at the restaurant at 7:10 p.m. Susan was waiting for me in the lobby. My first thought at seeing her was how gracefully she was aging. She's a couple of years younger than me and could easily pass for ten years younger. No gray hairs and a trim body. We ordered dinner and talked about our childhood and our parents. During our teenage days, she always chided me about being a neat freak, and I bugged her constantly about being sloppy. At the time, I felt protective of her and was apprehensive about her dating Dan Nelson, who was about four years older. He was almost finished with his undergraduate work and was soon to go to Harvard Law School.

The fish dinner was standard restaurant fare. Even though the restaurant was situated on the beach, the seafood was not fresh. Small disappointments build character. As we talked, the conversation drifted to Nelson, and Susan said, "I know you thought I really fell for Dan during the time I dated him. He was just a date, regardless of what he may have told you about our relationship. To be perfectly honest, I've always thought of Dan as a shallow person who would do anything to achieve financial success. He wrote me a letter once while he was at Harvard Law and bragged about his friendship with a Mafia-connected guy he had met at school and how connections with people like that could prove to be quite valuable. I think he got an adrenaline rush by associating with criminals. Frankly, Harry, I've never understood why you were friends. You're just about his opposite. You always take the high road on an issue, and he always looks for an angle to beat the system."

I was beginning to see Nelson in the way Susan had described him. There was a ring of truth to what she said about Nelson. On the other hand, I didn't feel like I had taken the high road on this investigation and it was bugging me. Susan's comment focused that fact sharply. I held back the urge to tell her how my ego had blocked access to the high road in this case. Character flaws are hard to admit from the top of a pedestal.

We said our good-byes, promised to keep in contact, and I headed back to Silicon Valley. It was 11:00 p.m. when I arrived at my hotel. On the way through the lobby, the desk clerk handed me a sealed, unmarked envelope. I tapped the end of the envelope on the counter and carefully tore off the top quarter inch and shook out a letter-sized piece of paper that looked as though it came from a computer printer. There was just one type-written line on the paper. 'Dante's Bar at midnight.' It read like a line from a 'B' movie. Whoever left the note had a flair for the dramatic. I asked the desk clerk when the envelope was delivered and if he could describe the person who left it.

"I think she brought it in about 10:00 p.m., and I believe she was wearing leather pants and jacket like a motorcycle rider."

"Did you remember anything about her face or hair? Was she heavy, thin, medium…What?"

"Now that you mention it, she was kind of heavy and wore black lipstick. I didn't see her for more that a few seconds, so that's the best I can do."

"Your powers of observation are remarkable." I said this tongue-in-cheek, but the clerk accepted it at face value. I hoped he wasn't expecting a tip. At least I knew it was a female who left the note, and from the description, it could have been Gina. I proceeded to Dante's bar, with extreme caution.

Dante's is attached to a family restaurant located on the El Camino Real in Mountain View. The restaurant serves a good breakfast and appears to be clean but the bar, like all bars, has the stench of stale beer and cigarettes.

Regulars hang out in the bar during the day. A more transient crowd fills the place at night.

I was all eyes when I entered the parking lot. Someone may not want me to remember seeing the money being printed. I looked at every car in the lot trying to spot a bad guy in waiting. Nothing. I felt sure I was being watched and was self-conscious walking from the car to the entrance of the bar. It was five minutes after midnight when I entered the bar. An overweight woman with a whiskey tenor voice, wearing a red, low-cut blouse, and black slacks was playing an out-of-tune piano while she bantered with the customers. An ashtray on the piano spewed a double tailed silky thread of smoke into the hazy blue light of the bar. There was a sign on the entrance door that said "No Smoking". Obviously for the benefit of the city health inspector. There were two empty seats at the long 'L' shaped bar. Six tables, all full, surrounded the small dance floor. The din of conversation made it impossible to hear the piano melody. Just tinkling high notes without reference to a rhythm. The male bartender had the leathery skin of a heavy smoker and the bony build of someone who drinks more than he eats. He glanced at me as I squeezed on to an empty bar stool. Looking toward the piano player, I sensed someone brush by to sit on the stool next to me. I looked to my side. It was Gina. She was looking at me as though she was an old acquaintance even though she had never made an effort to speak to me in Nelson's office. A little surprised and a little irritated I said,

"So what's the big mystery? I had the distinct feeling I wasn't your kind of guy."

I was actually thinking, *you never know what's coming next.* Gina had a worried look and leaned close while squeezing my right arm, making me feel the sharpness of her long, red acrylic finger nails. Her voice was shrill as she tried to talk above the noise.

"I know I shouldn't be here but a few things have happened to me in the past two days that scared the hell out of me. I need your help, and I think I can help you."

She really had my attention. I had a gut feeling about her detachment in the office. The way she was always too busy to speak, and always with the earphones like she was listening to music while she did her typing. Instead of playing into her 'damsel-in-distress' act I said, " I don't know how I could possibly help you. Maybe if you tell me what you can do for me, something will come to mind."

Gina looked around the room as though someone might be watching her. She said in a pleading voice, "Can we go outside where we can talk privately?"

I dropped a five-dollar bill on the bar, stood up and headed for the front door. Gina was following close. When we were outside we walked side-by-side to my rental car. I unlocked the passenger door first and waited for her to get in. After settling behind the wheel, I turned my body sideways on the seat and said, "Okay Gina. What is it you want me to know?"

She sat with her back to the door so she could face me. Her breasts were overflowing from her too tight blouse and were heaving as she began to breathe rapidly in anticipation of what she was about to tell me. I could smell her perfume, and cigarette breath.

"I have ways of finding out some important things at the office. My boyfriend talked me into doing it, so I did it and now I don't know what to do." Her brow was furrowed and her eyes showed three whites. I learned long ago that white showing on both sides and under the pupil is body language for, 'I'm scared out of my mind.'

In a calming voice I said, "Hold on. What are you talking about? Take it slow and tell me what you've been doing at the request of your boyfriend."

"Okay, I'm sorry. It's just that I'm really scared. I have to get away from him. If he finds out I'm talking to you it's my ass, and I'm sorry, but it's probably your ass too, if he finds out."

I was getting irritated at her inability to focus. "Damn it Gina, tell me what you came here to say. Don't worry about whose ass it is if he finds out. Do you even know why I came to California?"

Gina swallowed hard and tried to compose herself. I could tell by her reaction to what I just said that she was in the habit of subjugating herself to men. She was excited but her breathing had calmed a little.

She looked me square in the eyes and said, "I know you came out here to deliver U.S. currency paper to Theodore Martin so he could make counterfeit money using the copy machine he invented."

She took a breath and waited for my reaction. I was in mild shock that she knew I had delivered currency paper to Martin, but I didn't show a reaction. She continued, "I also know that Dan and a guy back in Florida are involved with the counterfeiting plot that's going on. But, so help me God, I didn't have any idea someone would be killed over it. Now I don't know what'll happen next, and I'm afraid to go to the cops because, if Leon finds out, he'll kill me.

Another pause, but this time to calm herself instead of looking for my reaction. She continued, "He's crazy when it comes to that bunch of survivalist assholes he runs with. They think they're into some kind of high-minded political philosophy. They talk about saving us all from the federal government by doing all kinds of violent stuff. Let me tell you, I wouldn't put anything past these guys. I thought it was all talk until I got pressured into getting Leon some information. I made the mistake of telling him that I overheard a conversation between Dan and Martin about the machine Martin had invented. I told him Martin's machine could copy anything so good that you can't tell the copy from the original, and that he wanted Dan to handle the patent application for him.

Gina stopped for a moment and gave me a look that told me she was about to drop some real important news on me. She took a deep breath and continued, "Leon's group is strapped for money and will do just about anything to make a buck. So, when Leon hears about Martin's copy machine, he goes ape-shit. He told his buddies, and the bunch of them hatched a plan that, among other things, involved me getting information for them. The group has ten members and they call themselves the Peninsula Coast Citizens Militia. They're scary as hell. They're true believers, and they'll do anything for the cause. They talk about ultimately overthrowing the federal government and they talk with other militia groups around the country to share ideas. Hell, in California alone, over twenty-five militia groups have sprung up in the past several years. I heard them talking about how cool they thought a militia group in Michigan was for supporting the bombing of the Federal Building in Oklahoma City. I knew this was some scary shit that I didn't want any part of. I couldn't get myself to break off with Leon. Just the way I am. One thing led to another and before long I knew about the scheme to use the machine to make counterfeit money. I knew the currency paper was being couried to Martin from Florida."

I wondered how the hell she discovered all those private little things. Something I would determine later. By way of satisfying her 'quid pro quo' approach, I could get her off the hook by finding the group's hangout along with the money machine and paper. I could then alert the local PD to the tie-in with Martin's murder, and voila, they all go to the joint, and Gina is clear. However, things in real life are never so simple. But, at the moment it was the only path I could think of taking so I said, "Where do you think the militia would keep the copy machines and paper, assuming they took them."

Gina looked at me as though I was a co-conspirator who had just bought into the crime. Her manner became quiet and reflective. She said, "Most of the guys in the group are just regular working types who have wives, children, and mortgages. They could hide the stuff at any one of the their houses. But Leon lives alone in the loft of an old fish warehouse over at Pillar Point near Half Moon Bay. Hiding the machines there would eliminate the wives and children of some family finding out what's going on. He's got plenty of room to hold the machines and paper. He drives a white Ford pick-up truck that he parks on the west side of the warehouse near the stairs that go up to the loft where he lives. Check his place first. Because of me putting them on to the copy machine information, this crazy-ass counterfeit scheme is more or less his responsibility in the group, and he would more than likely take the paper and stuff to his place. Here's his address."

Gina had taken a pen and small notebook from her purse and wrote Leon's address. She tore the page away from the notebook and handed it to me. In spite of her coarse looks, and an in-your-face attitude, Gina appeared to be somewhat organized and capable of logical thought. Minimal requirements for working in an attorney's office. She continued, "If you can help bust this thing up without involving me, I'll help you all I can. Maybe if they sent them all to jail I can get away from Leon. I just don't want to get involved with the police or have Leon find out I'm going against him in this thing. "

This was a proposition that sounded like trouble for me. Radical militia-group people are scary. I could just call it quits without giving Nelson back any of his retainer and go get my boat. I didn't owe Nelson anything, however, it did bother me that he might get his avaricious ass killed by Gina's friends. I wouldn't make any more money if I stayed to help Nelson and Gina, but some things I do, I write off as being my contribution to a moral society. It makes me feel good. Some things I know I'm going to do, regardless of the thought processes I grind myself through prior to doing the act. Like when I'm on a diet and decide to take a run along a route that takes me by a fast food joint. Even though I tell myself I'll just run past, I know deep down, I'm stopping for a burger, fries, and coke. Make that a diet coke. I said, "Okay Gina, I'll help you. The first thing I want you to do is take me to your office so I can read the files Nelson has on Martin and the copy machine. I assume you have a key to the office."

"Hell yes, I have a key. Sometimes I have to work on weekends and evenings." Then she added with lower volume, "Sometimes I hate that damn job."

Gina drove her car to the office. I followed in my rental car. It was approximately 1:00 a.m. when we arrived. Gina walked up the stairs to the front door of the office suite. She opened the door, walked in, and before she turned on the lights I signaled her to wait a second while I walked into Nelson's office and closed the vertical blinds in case someone got nosy. I said, "So, where are the active files?"

Gina pointed me to Nelson's active file storage cabinet. He had ten or twelve files sorted in alphabetical order. Martin's file was the thickest, mostly boilerplate stuff about the patent application along with a physical description of the invention. It appeared that in addition to claiming the highest resolution of copying ever invented, Martin's invention embodied the significant feature of being able to infuse holograms and other types of images below the surface of a variety of materials. The device had the capability of very high magnification and the ability to use the greatly magnified image to faithfully reproduce the original. It read like science fiction. The documents described the process in mathematical terms and I didn't have a clue what they were talking about. There was also text that was full of terms that could only be understood by a xerography expert. A document inserted into the file in front of the patent application indicated that a temporary patent had been granted and that a year would pass before the patent would be permanent. The document was dated July 27, 1997. Martin's name was the only name on the application. SRI, his employer at the time he developed the machine, was not mentioned.

 I went to the desk and tried the drawers. They were unlocked. In the lower left hand drawer, I found a letter-sized plain white envelope taped to the backside of the end of the drawer. The envelope had a solid object inside that proved to be an 8mm tape, the type you use in a video camera. On the end of the tape cassette was a white label with the words Martin/Kincaid dated eight months ago on 05 March. I knew what was on the tape. This was the smoking gun.

 I pocketed the tape and continued to search Nelson's office for a VHS tape that would have been copied from the 8mm tape. No luck. Attorneys usually do not take possession of a tape from an investigator until the contents of the tape become an issue in court or, because of the tape's content; the attorney knows he can pressure the other side into a favorable settlement without a court appearance.

There was no litigation involved here. Nelson wanted to have possession of the tape for another reason. He may have made a VHS copy that he sent, or personally gave to Martin at the time he put the blackmail scheme into operation.

It was 1:40 a.m. Gina was standing near her desk looking a little scared. I was rummaging through Nelson's files. To make conversation, I said, "I'll bet you enjoy working with Bonnie. It looks like she keeps things in shipshape around here. Does she do the filing?"

"Yeah. She's real efficient, but I think she gets pissed off if I get too close to Dan because I think she wants to sleep with him. I doubt Dan digs older women."

I dropped the subject thinking it was a stretch since Bonnie is just about old enough to be Nelson's mother. Who knows though, it could be her fantasy about a last fling since she still appeared to be in good shape.

After putting things back into place I turned from behind the desk and accidentally dropped my pen. It rolled under and to the back of Nelson's desk. I bent over to pick it up and noticed a thread hanging down from behind the desk drawer. The thread was connected to the underside of the desktop. I looked out at Gina's desk just as she was walking out of the office door into the hallway. I assumed she was on her way to the rest room.

On her way out of the door, Gina yelled, "hold the fort, nature calls."

I got on my knees and crawled under the desk. The string was a thread from a strip of book binding tape that was holding a small FM transmitter firmly to the underside of the desk. The transmitter was a 1-inch square printed circuit board with a number of very small electronic parts soldered to it. An antenna wire was connected to the printed circuit board and was taped to the underside of the desk for a length of about two feet. I'd seen many like it, and they were all imported from the U.K. or Germany. This type of transmitter has a range of one city block, providing there is no interference by buildings or hills. It uses the FM band and transmits continually until the battery is used up. The manufacturer usually sets the transmitter frequency to 108 Mhz, the top of the FM radio band. The PC board was connected to a 9-volt battery and the two components were taped together with black plastic tape. The whole package was taped to the underside of the desk with book binding tape. The transmitter had been under the desk long enough to collect a layer of dust and possibly long enough that the battery had to have been changed at least once. Likely one of the tasks Gina did during an evening or weekend work session. I left the taped-up transmitter in place and came out from under the desk. Gina came back into the office just as I was walking from Nelson's office to her desk. Her upper left desk drawer was open, and I walked over to take a look. Before I could suggest leaving, I caught a glimpse of a small AM/FM radio with a headset attached. I picked it up and said to Gina, "Does this thing get good reception in the office?"

The radio was tuned to 108 Mhz on the FM dial. Gina's face reddened. "Yeah, it's great, I just put on the earphones and turn it on. Never even have to tune it." She had a smirk on her face that looked like she was thinking 'I'm so cool for telling you about the radio that I use daily to listen to Nelson's conversations.'

Tacitly understanding what Leon had Gina do for him, I put the radio away, shut off the lights, opened the vertical binds and left the office with Gina walking directly behind me. After locking the door we walked down the stairs side by side and onto the sidewalk. Both of our cars were parked in front of the building. I thanked Gina for her help, got into my car and made a 'U'-turn to head back to the hotel.

In the rear view mirror I saw Gina's car pull away from the curb and make a right turn. At the same time, in the rear view mirror, I saw headlights pulling away from the curb one block down the street from Nelson's office in front of the Town Bar. The lighted sign over the bar's entrance went out as I noticed the vehicle pulling away from the curb, and turning left onto the same street Gina had taken.

11

I got back to the hotel at 1:55 a.m. The place was a ghost town. My room was quiet and cool. I undressed quickly and fell into bed, falling asleep in the time it took for two fat sheep to jump a couple of desks that looked like radios.

It was 8:00 a.m. Friday when I woke to the radio playing a thirty-year-old Blue Mitchell recording. I couldn't think of a more pleasant note on which to start the day. By the time I was ready to hit the streets it was 8:50 a.m. I was obligated to Nelson through Saturday. It was up for grabs after that. I made a mental note to contact Bonnie this morning and get the time and flight number for my return to Daytona Beach on Sunday, providing the Sheriff's office said I could go. It bugged me that I may have to leave the area without knowing who whacked Martin and what happened to the bogus-buck making system. I went across the street for breakfast and picked up a copy of the San Jose News from the vending machine outside of the restaurant.

The local news section had a lead story of a shooting that occurred in Mountain View at 1:55 a.m. The victim was identified by a neighbor as Gina Wilson. The hair was standing up on the back of my neck. The story stated that Gina Wilson was murdered early Friday morning and that the police were interviewing neighbors in an attempt to find a suspect. A neighbor in Gina's apartment complex had told police that she had heard several shots at 1:55 a.m., followed by the sound of squealing tires. According to the story, the neighbor then looked out her window and saw Gina lying near her car in the apartment parking lot. The story identified Gina as a legal secretary who worked for a Mountain View attorney. Nelson's name was not mentioned. There were no suspects at the time the police were questioned about the incident.

I felt the familiar tingling shoot through my stomach, which, by the way was still empty. I sat in the booth staring at the paper feeling certain that I could have prevented her death had I followed the car that took off after her last night. The article threw me for a loop. I changed my mind about eating, threw a buck on the table and went back to the hotel.

Nelson answered his office phone sounding depressed. When I identified myself, he said in a more positive sounding voice, "Harry, where the hell have you been? I've been waiting to hear from you. Do you know about Gina?"

"Yeah, I read the papers. What's your take on it?"

"It's got to be connected with Martin. Maybe she knew something about the money and someone else knew she was ready to talk about it. Hell, I don't know. What's your take on it?"

Sidestepping the issue of Gina being murdered, I quietly said, "Were you blackmailing Martin?" I could almost hear Nelson's shock in the silence.

"Why the hell would I do that?"

"If I were a cop looking for a suspect, I would think that maybe it was your way of getting Martin to print the money for you and yours. Not to mention that two people get whacked that have a connection to you through your law office. Is Zucker your partner in this mess?" I couldn't wait for his answer to that question.

"Damn it Harry, I told you, I don't have any idea what Martin was up to. Get off my back." I interpreted his answer to my question as a no.

"How's Bonnie taking it?"

"I might just as well close the place down for a few days. We're both devastated."

"How come you don't have your office secure from eavesdropping?"

"What makes you think my office is not secure? What? Do you think Gina had something to do with compromising client information?"

Continuing my quasi interrogation I said, "You're going to screw around and get yourself killed. Did you ever meet Gina's boyfriend?"

"Yeah, he was in the office one time, briefly, and I had the impression he couldn't wait to leave. He looked nervous. I guess it was because he didn't expect to see me. It was after hours. Gina was working overtime, and I dropped in to see how it was going for her. Do you think she knew about Martin's counterfeit scheme? Give me a break, Harry, you're acting like an amateur detective."

"I don't *think* she knew about it, I *know* she did. She told me she passed information on to her boyfriend about Martin's invention and the paper being sent out here. Scare you, Dan?" Do you still deny that you're in this thing with Zucker?"

Nelson was silent for several seconds. I could sense his shock at knowing his most cherished secret had been blown. I wondered which of the private conversations he worried about the most.

I broke the silence by saying, "Looks like I pushed a button. Why don't you tell me about it."

I could hear a scuffling sound and imagined Nelson's hand going to his face, massaging the end of his nose. Without any mention of how Gina got the information, he said, "Quit talking down to me Harry. Gina's death has me shook up."

He was being defensive, and I decided to turn the screw. I said, "Gina knew the paper was being shipped to Martin and that I was delivering it. She got that information from hearing you talk about it, probably to Zucker. We're way past your concocted story that you were just doing Zucker a favor. You'd be wise to let me know what the hell's going on before you're forced to 'fess up' to the Sheriff's Department."

I could hear Nelson's breath go out of him and he said in a defeated sounding, deadpan voice, "Just finish the investigation I paid you to do. Send me a report of your findings and then drop it. I'll take it from there. Okay Harry?"

He wanted me out of his hair. He looked guilty as hell and I was not going to offer him any protection. I said, "You got it." I hung up the phone feeling unburdened.

I called Bonnie immediately after talking to Nelson. She was not in the office. Thinking she would leave me a message sometime today, I didn't worry about getting in touch with her. I grabbed my binoculars, a note pad, and pointed the car toward Pillar Point. I stopped at a discount department store before leaving Mountain View and picked up three long sleeved knit shirts, a light weight jogging jacket, a bag of three pairs of socks, and a bag of three pairs of underwear. I packed assuming I would be back in Daytona Beach late Wednesday night or early Thursday morning. Assuming will get you into trouble. The rust was falling off.

The important thing was that I had now known about the counterfeiting operation, without reporting it, for about thirty-five hours.

12

Pillar Point is a small fishing village located halfway between Santa Cruz and San Francisco at the northern tip of Half Moon Bay. A large marina, a string of boat yards, fresh fish retailers, and an abandoned cannery occupy the shoreline of this ruggedly picturesque coastal town. The military maintains a radar station at the tip of land called Pillar Point. For security reasons, it's off-limits to the public. The address Gina jotted down belonged to the abandoned cannery. It was a two-story green building sitting out over the water on stilts. A one-lane-wide ramp led up to a wharf of the same width that ran along the west side of the cannery. There were no vehicles on the wharf. I found a parking spot at the boat yard next door to the cannery and walked out to the end of the wharf, stepping over snails on the way. I crunched several of them before noticing they were just about everywhere there was shade. Leon Suggs' name reminded me of a snail.

There was a door leading into a stairwell that was attached to the outside of the building. The door was closed but unlocked. The doorframe was splintered at the locking mechanism. I walked to the top of the stairs where an open archway led to a room that was part office and part living room. An adjoining room, elevated by two steps and containing a double bed, looked out to the south, onto Half Moon Bay. It looked as though the adjoining room was where the one-time bosses of the cannery watched the fishing boats unload their catches onto the main floor of the cannery.

I checked the papers lying on the desk in the makeshift living room and found several recent documents with Leon Suggs' name and address on them. It was easy to see that Suggs did not have the machines or paper in his living quarters. I quickly went downstairs in search of an entrance to the cannery and found one at the end of the building facing the bay. The main floor of the building was empty except for several completely rusted pieces of machinery and a hellish looking black motorcycle painted with red skulls and flames flashing back behind the high rise handle bars.

I could picture Gina sitting on the small cushioned seat atop the rear fender. She was big enough that the seat would have fit her like a thong.

There were no walled off rooms on the main floor. I could see the entire building and it was clear that there were no secret hiding places or hidden treasures here. I was pressing my luck just being in the building, so I left and started back to shore along the wharf.

I was halfway to shore when a white pickup truck bounded up the ramp onto the wharf. My internal alarm went off. I feigned a tourist look; interested but unconcerned.

The pickup swerved toward the warehouse and stopped abruptly with a jerking motion, at an angle, in front of me. The driver bolted out of the truck, slammed the door and stomped to the front of the truck. He stood alongside the warehouse facing me.

He was about six-two, lean, and had greasy, scraggly hair tied in a ponytail and a mousy-brown-colored bushy beard. A grease smudged red headband kept the hair out of his face. He wore jeans that were stained with oil and grease, a sleeveless dirty black leather vest with no undershirt, and carried a set of keys on his belt that made him sound like a cowboy with spurs when he walked. His beat-up black work boots had a chrome chain over each instep. His fingernails were rimmed with black. His right forearm had tattoos of a large dagger with a drop of blood dripping into the eye of a skull. His right upper arm displayed a nude female doing the splits. A snake, a fire breathing dragon, and a Harley emblem decorated his left arm. When he was three feet from me I could smell his dank, oil, gas, and grease odor mixed with B.O. Gina could really pick classy guys.

In good biker syntax he said, "What you fuckin' doing at my house, brother?"

I could see there was not going to be much reasoning with this guy, so I tried to lighten up the situation. "Just seeing the sights, brother."

"This is private property, dickhead. Not a fuckin tourist attraction. He moved toward me. He had a wild-eyed look that I had seen many times just before the violence started. His fists and teeth were clenched. He kicked a rusty five-gallon bucket that was in his way, causing it to crash against the warehouse. A psychopath if ever I saw one. I said, "Whoa boss. I didn't do anything. I'm just sightseeing."

"I don't like people poking around my private stuff and I'm gonna kick your fuckin'-ass so you don't forget and maybe think of coming back for another visit."

My fight or flight instinct was now one hundred percent turned on, but he had blocked my way. Flight was not an option. He lunged at me throwing a right at the middle of my face. I side stepped the punch and buried my right fist into his midsection. The punch caught him by surprise and he fell to his knees, gasping for air. On his way down, I caught the side of his face with the full force of my left forearm, and drove him into the deck.

Thinking I should take the opportunity to split, I turned to my right to go between the truck and the warehouse, but before I could take two steps, he tackled me around the legs. I fell to the ground and tried to kick him off of me. No good. He evidently got his breath back because the next thing I knew I smelled it as I looked into his face. Sour smoke, onions, and garlic. He had me pinned by the neck and was cocking his right hand and arm to bash in my face. I brought my knee up with all the speed and power I could muster and caught him full force between his legs, all the way to the bone. His right hand missed its target, smashing into the wharf as he rolled off onto his side, in the fetal position.

I stood up. My heart was pounding. I was breathing hard. I resisted a very strong urge to kick his face in. Instead I stepped back and said, "Had enough, tough guy?"

He was still in the fetal position, moaning. One hand clutching his crotch and the other lying motionless. Through clenched teeth he grunted, "I'm gonna cut you to ribbons, son-of-a-bitch."

"Don't you ever stop playing tough guy? According to Gina you're big on beating up women, but you ought to rethink messing with guys your size."

That was a stretch, because he was a couple of inches taller and at least ten years younger. He was staring up at me quizzically. The mention of Gina was causing him to think, probably for the first time today. He got to his knees, took a couple of deep breaths, and then began to get to his feet, still holding his crotch and letting his right arm hang loose at his side. I was ready but he didn't look like he was still in the mood for a fight. I could see a large knife sheathed on the inside of his right boot as he climbed to his feet.

I pushed him over and grabbed the knife from his boot before he was all the way up. I slammed my right foot down on his head. I let a few seconds go by and then released his head and stepped aside with the knife extended in front of me in my right hand. He slowly got to his feet, continued to hold his crotch and looked at me with sizzling hate.

"Who the hell are you?" Suggs said wincing in pain and holding his right wrist in his left hand.

"Just a guy trying to find some answers. I assume you're Leon Suggs."

"Yeah, that's right and don't think you don't have to tell me what you're doing at my house, motherfucker. How you know about Gina?"

I let the question go unanswered. Maybe he would tell me what I was doing at his house. I said, "We crossed paths recently and she mentioned you."

"I'll take care of her ass the next time I see her. And if you see her again, I'll take care of your ass too. Know what I'm saying?"

It was big talk for a loser but I knew what he was saying. He didn't appear to know about Gina, which means he didn't have anything to do with her murder and he doesn't read the morning paper. With no lack of respect for the dead I was not feeling unhappy about breaking the news about Gina.

"I don't think you'll be taking care of Gina the next time you see her. When was the last time you saw her?"

"Day before yesterday. Why?"

"You weren't in Mountain View around 2:00 a.m. this morning?"

Suggs' eyes were beginning to get big.

"Fuck no. Who are you?"

"Harry Caine, I'm investigating the murder of Theodore Martin." I'm sure Suggs thought I was a cop who was going to nail him for something. The color drained out of his face.

"Gina told me something about it, but what the hell does it have to do with me?"

"Don't you read the paper?"

"Nothing to read in the morning paper but a bunch of liberal bullshit and I've had my fill of that. This whole fuckin' country is filling up with liberal bullshit. Know what I'm saying?"

I knew what he was saying. It was the party line for all the survivalist type radicals that have become part of militias across the country. I said, "Gina was murdered. Shot to death. It happened early this morning in the parking lot at her apartment house."

He looked like he was going to faint. His hands went slack, his lower lip started to quiver and his eyes teared up. He was clearly torn up. I didn't like admitting it to myself but I felt for the guy. His acquired tough guy shell had been stripped.

In a weak voice, Suggs said, "I don't know what the hell's going on with all this shit. We didn't lay a hand on Martin and we sure as hell didn't want anything to happen to Gina. She probably thought I was tough on her but I loved her. God!"

I let a few seconds go by and decided to give him a chance to unload.

"I know what you and Gina were up to."

Suggs' face took on a resigned look. He said, "Okay I don't fuckin' want any more trouble than I already have. I guess we went a little nuts when Gina told us about the printing machine. I gave her a bug and told her how to hook it up and change the battery. Hell, Martin was the guy doing the crime. We didn't print the fuckin' money. We just wanted to get some of it for the group. We didn't figure we could get hassled ripping off a scumbag criminal. Who the fuck would turn us in?" Suggs looked at the ground and began repeating the word, God, over and over.

"I take it when you say "us," you mean your militia group?"

"Yeah." Suggs was looking straight ahead with the unfocused look of a person who was totally inside his own mind. His speech was just as unfocused, and he said, "If Bonnie hadn't told us, we wouldn't of known about the paper coming out here. When we found that out, we made plans to steal the money and the machines. We never got to do it, because we never found out where he was doing the fuckin' printing."

I interrupted, "The info about the money paper and the plan to print the stuff came from Bonnie, not Nelson?"

Suggs' eyes regained their focused look as he put me in his line of sight. "Yeah, that's right, stupid. And we found out about Martin's invention from Gina listening to Nelson and Martin talking in Nelson's office. Shit man, I know how to find out about anything and how to take care of nosy bastards like you. You're damn lucky you ain't floating face down under this fuckin' dock."

Suggs' anger was ebbing and I tried to refocus him on what Gina had done for his group. I said, "Specifically, how did Gina know about the currency paper being shipped here?"

"Now how the fuck do you suppose, Mr. Detective? She listened in on Bonnie's phone calls by usin' a headset that could button switch to any line in the office. We thought Bonnie and Nelson were doing the thing together. Bonnie was just taking care of the fuckin' details for that asshole, Nelson."

Suggs stopped talking and stared into space for a few seconds, and then said, "I'm through with this shit man."

From out of nowhere Suggs looked like a wild man again. His fists and teeth were clenched as he spit out the words, "Tell me where they took her you son-of-a-bitch!"

Suggs' world had temporarily crashed, and it looked like he was trying to hold on to the anger and rage that he had learned to feel comfortable with. Out of some possibly misguided sympathy, I thought the least I could do was to tell him how to get to the Santa Clara County Coroner's office. Without going inside, Suggs walked to his truck spewing expletives, and kicked a large dent in the driver's side door. He jumped in, slammed the door, backed off the wharf at high speed, and was gone.

I walked to the edge of the wharf. The adrenalin rush was subsiding but my hands were shaking. I felt sore, a little shook up, but exhilerated over my victory. I gently dropped the knife.

13

I went back to the hotel to research Bonnie who, after my conversation with Suggs, now looked like the linchpin figure in the operation. It appeared that no one except Gina, Leon's group, and I knew of the militia's plan to steal the money. I was convinced the militia group did not steal the machines and paper and that left Bonnie. It was clear that I needed to know more about her.

The nameplate at the front of her desk was Bonnie Bliss. I didn't know if it was her maiden name or her last married name. That, and the fact that she didn't wear a wedding band, was all I knew about her. I ran a name search using Bonnie Bliss and picked up her social security number and current address in Mountain View. Using her social security number, I obtained several names that were associated with her number at some time. The first being

Bonnie Bliskowski. My stomach felt the old electric shock when, near the bottom of the list, I saw the name of Bonnie Zucker. The fifteen-year-old address was in Newark, New Jersey. My immediate thought was that Moshe Zucker was previously married to Bonnie. It took two microseconds to realize that it was more likely that Bonnie was either Moshe Zucker's mother or that it was just a coincidence that her last name used to be Zucker. My gut told me to forget the coincidence theory.

I asked the information operator to connect me to the vital statistics records section of the County Hall of Records in the same county as Newark, New Jersey. After telling her what a great voice she had, and my wish to visit Newark someday, the Essex County Hall of Records Clerk did a marriage records search using the name of Bonnie Bliss. There were no records for Bonnie Bliss. I remembered seeing a Jr. attached to Zucker's name on his Harvard diploma, so I asked the clerk to search the marriage records for a Moshe Zucker. After a few moments the clerk found a record of Moshe Zucker marrying Bonnie Bliskowski forty-five years ago in a justice of the peace ceremony in Cedar Grove, New Jersey. The clerk was so accommodating that I didn't hesitate asking whether or not a birth record existed for Moshe Zucker, Jr. from about forty-three or forty-four years ago. The cheerful clerk put me on hold while I listened to the theme from the movie Arthur, thinking that the line about getting stuck between the moon and New York City would make a good theme song for a hit man who uses a knife. The clerk returned in a few moments and told me that Moshe Zucker, Jr. was born to Bonnie Zucker and Moshe Zucker, Sr. forty-four years ago in October. She wanted to give me all the particulars but I had all the info I needed. I thanked her profusely and promised her a dinner the next time I was in Newark. She giggled, and we said goodbye.

    I called the operator and asked to be connected to the clerk of the Essex County Civil Court in Newark, New Jersey. After a litany of instructions and explanations I was connected to the clerk's office. I sensed that sweetness and flattery would work to my disadvantage with this lady. To ward off a possible refusal to do a search over the telephone, I used my most polite and humble voice to request a search of the civil index for the past twenty years on Moshe Zucker or Moshe Zucker, Sr. The clerk, in a very business like manner, put me on hold. Two minutes later the clerk informed me that there was one fifteen-year-old divorce case with the respondent being Bonnie Zucker and the petitioner being Moshe Zucker, Sr. I was given the case number and offered the names of the attorneys involved. I didn't need the names of the attorneys, but took the case number, and light heartedly promised another dinner if I ever got to Newark. The promise fell on unresponsive ears.

    I now knew Bonnie was boat-yard Zucker's mother. They say you don't have to look very far to find a connection among people, and they're right. I imagined that Bonnie probably moved to California some years after the divorce to start a new life, and her son connected her with Nelson. Nelson hired her and she became indispensable to him. Bonnie, keeping in touch with her son the way mothers do, was probably Zucker's prime candidate to carry out the plan that was born when Nelson casually told him about Martin's invention. Or, Zucker, Jr. could have told his dad about his plan and his dad was instrumental in getting Bonnie to help carry it out. But why would Zucker Sr. believe Bonnie would get involved at all? Why should she? And why would a son ask his mother to assist in carrying out a crime. After all, here was a respectable woman leading, what looked like, a respectable life.

I didn't have all the information I needed about the past life of the Zucker's, especially Bonnie Zucker.

I called a 'court-runner' company in Dallas that has a network of runners in all major U.S. cities, and requested an uncertified copy of the entire file identified by the case number provided by the clerk of the Newark court. For an increased fee, which I would bill to Nelson, the Dallas court runner company promised to send me the file by FedEx to be delivered by 10:00 a.m. tomorrow morning. American ingenuity is awesome. In the meantime I decided to go over to Nelson's office and talk with Bonnie.

When I arrived, Bonnie was alone in the office looking busy as always. I gave her my condolences and said, "Gina thought highly of you. I guess you were like a mentor to her."

"Well maybe. Gina was a hard person to get to know. But I'll tell you one thing, she was way off base to think I was sexually interested in Dan. He's young enough to be my son."

A bell went off in my head, but being intent on opening the topic of boat-yard Zucker being her son, I dismissed the alarm. I said, "Coincidentally, are Nelson and your son friends?

"Well," Bonnie said tentatively. "Yes, they are. In fact it was my son, 'Mo', who helped get me a job with Dan when I first moved to California. It worked out well for me, and for Dan."

"Your son is Moshe Zucker, right?" I said as a matter of innocent discovery, "I've heard Nelson mention his name in relation to Harvard Law School. I guess you know it was your son who sent me here to deliver some packages to Theodore Martin. Small world, eh?"

"Mo never mentioned that you were making a delivery to Mr. Martin. But I haven't spoken with him for a few weeks now."

"Why did you move to California, I mean after living on the east coast for so many years?"

"One of those things," Bonnie said. "My marriage hit a storm we couldn't weather and down it went. After kicking around Newark for several years, I decided to move away and get a fresh start. I always thought of California as a place where people went to get a fresh start. So here I am. I never dreamed it would be so expensive to live here, but I make ends meet. Dan has been a great friend, and a good employer."

From what she said I got the impression that she basically lived hand to mouth, but was happy with the arrangement. In an effort to keep her talking I said, "Yeah, I know what you mean. Nelson has a habit of succeeding and that's not a bad horse to tie your wagon to."

Bonnie looked at me quizzically, as though she just noticed something significant about me. She hesitated for a few seconds and added, "I want Mo to be successful, just like Dan, and if I have anything to do with it he will."

I could see the determination in her face. Her jaw became a little more square and her eyes more penetrating. Again there was the short reflection before she spoke, "There's little I can do to help Mo though. You know, kids grow up, and a parent's influence becomes less and less as time goes by. He's so intelligent and able. I hate to see him wasting himself in that boat yard."

"Why the boat yard in the first place?"

"Mo's father exerts considerable influence over him. He is the major shareholder in the Daytona Beach Boat Yard and wants someone he can trust to take care of the financial aspects of the business. I suppose Mo feels obligated. You know, the good son shtick."

If what Bonnie said was true, I wondered how the son escaped the 'me generation' modus operandi of his time. Bonnie made her son sound like a milk toast type of guy, which he wasn't. I guessed that boat-yard Zucker's basic conflict in life was that his self-image was out of whack with the way the rest of the world saw him. He either had to adjust his self-image or change the way the rest of the world sees him. A resolution to that kind of conflict can lead to desperate measures.

Changing the focus of the conversation I said, "You told me that Nelson hired Max Kincaid to look into the background of Theodore Martin. Do you suppose Nelson has Kincaid's report filed in his office?"

"I can't imagine why he wouldn't." Bonnie said.

"I know Nelson wouldn't mind me looking at it since I am working for him. Do you suppose you could dig it up for me?"

"I can't do that. Dan hired Kincaid without discussing the issue with me. He obviously didn't want me to have anything to do with it. I'm sure he had his reasons. I respect his privacy, and he respects mine. I'm sorry Mr. Caine."

"Yeah, well I'm sure you two have a lot of respect for each other, but in the interest of helping Nelson, I thought it would be a good idea to read what Kincaid wrote in his report. Do you know if there was a video tape associated with Kincaid's investigation of Martin?"

"I have no idea," Bonnie said defensively, as she began stroking the end of her nose with her index finger in the classic gesture that indicates stress and possible deception. "But if there was, I haven't seen it."

I didn't believe her and decided I would ask Nelson about his hiring Kincaid and what Kincaid had delivered. I thanked Bonnie for her information and told her to let Nelson know I'd be back to talk to him later in the afternoon.

I left the office with the feeling that the report was not there, but for some reason Bonnie wanted me to believe it was. It didn't appear that Zucker could have known about Gina's connection with the militia group's plans to make Martin's counterfeit operation their own. That left Bonnie as the connection between Zucker and the money.

I drove to Bonnie's house in Mountain View. The house was in an upscale neighborhood about three miles from Nelson's office. The well-maintained house sat on an equally well-maintained large corner lot. I guessed the current market value to be well over a million dollars, which is similar to a two hundred and fifty thousand dollar house in the suburban areas of Daytona Beach. Not a bad fresh start.

Knowing Bonnie was at her office, I didn't hesitate pulling into the driveway and parking in front of her double-car garage door. Without giving it a lot of thought, I was about to commit a felony in the name of justice. I knew it would be the most direct, and possibly the only way to find out what Bonnie was up to. I hoped the ends would justify the means. In this case, I was betting they would. That bit of rationalization didn't dispell the anxiety I felt as I walked to the front door and rang the bell. I let a few seconds go by and then said in a loud voice, "Okay, I'll go around to the side door." You never know who's watching.

The bushes at the side of the house afforded me the privacy to slip a credit card into the doorjamb. The deadbolt had not been engaged. It opened with little effort. The door connecting the kitchen to the garage was not locked. I slipped my shoes off at the kitchen door to avoid leaving shoe prints. The house was cool and quiet. The plush, dark-blue carpet silenced any footstep sounds as I walked down the hallway off the living room. I started my search in a converted bedroom that now housed an office. A two-drawer file cabinet sat next to a long table holding a desktop computer and a few other electronic goodies. The file cabinet was neatly arranged with all file folders labeled in alphabetical order. The report I was looking for was not in the file folders. I didn't see any other reasonable hiding places in the office. The master bedroom was at the end of the long hallway connecting the living area to the bed and bathroom areas of the house. A large, mirrored, double sliding door occupied the entire wall on one side of the room. I slid the door open and found a neatly ordered closet full of women's dresses, pants suits and shoes. The top shelf was empty, except for a cardboard box sitting at the far end.

 I pulled the box down and looked through a number of file folders, mostly having to do with past tax information. One folder, labeled 'MO', held a business-sized envelope containing fifteen hundred dollars in hundred-dollar bills. A real payday for your run-of-the-mill burglar. There was nothing else in the file folder except a sliver of ribbon stuck in one of the bottom corners of the box. I pulled on the ribbon, and, to my surprise, a false bottom lifted up exposing a legal sized manila envelope. I opened the unlabeled envelope and pulled out Max Kincaid's report regarding his background investigation of Theodore Martin.

 Was I right or was I right? I learned long ago to trust body language, as well as my own instincts. Bonnie lied about the report and now I wondered about the truth of the other things she told me. The report was addressed to Bonnie Bliss, which made her Kincaid's client. It was accompanied by an invoice for services rendered. The invoice was for sixteen hundred and thirty five dollars. The expenses, detailed separately from the hourly surveillance charges, included a covert camera, miniature VCR, 8mm videotape, and mileage charges.

The report contained six pages of narrative detailing Theodore Martin's activities for two days. The daily activities were delineated chronologically. I noticed Martin visited the porn shop next door to his 'PMS' store front office on each of the two nights. The narrative regarding the second night of surveillance detailed Martin's visit to the porn shop in graphic detail, as Kincaid had told me. The report stated that the videotape was enclosed. To be exact, it was now enclosed in my pocket, not in the envelope.

Bonnie had apparently planted Kincaid's tape of Martin in Nelson's desk, setting him up to take the fall for Martin's murder. She apparently had Kincaid tell me that he had given the tape to Nelson. Kincaid would lie about anything, given the right amount of money.

I did a systematic but unproductive search of the house for a gun. I had no information on the caliber of weapon used to shoot Martin or Gina, but I was betting the same weapon was used in both killings. During the search I found love letters from Anthony Falcon to Bonnie. One of the letters talked about Falcon being under the thumb of Zucker, Sr. in New Jersey. I imagined that Zucker Sr. let Falcon off the hook for banging his wife, in trade for future favors, in lieu of whacking him, which would be the standard punishment for such behavior in Moshe Zucker's world. There were also telephone records listing calls to Zucker at the Daytona Beach Boat Yard and repeated calls to a number in Fernandina Beach, Florida, that I guessed belonged to Falcon.

I copied Kincaid's report and Bonnie's toll call records on her office fax machine, put everything back where I found it, and left the house.

14

On the way back to the hotel, I went through the same reasoning I had used before doing the B&E. The process took the edge off my anxiety. I was carrying a copy of Kincaid's report, Bonnie's phone records and the 8mm videotape I found in Nelson's desk. It was all evidence and I was withholding it. It has never ceased to amaze me how fast I can go from a low-key, hum-drum existence, to being in big trouble. I knew I should go to the Sheriff's Office with the information, but I first wanted to have enough evidence to make a tight case against the bad guys. Who was I kidding? The real reason had to do with an ego trip. Guess whose?

I called Detective Clark from my room at 4:30 p.m. Not to turn over all my goodies to him, but just to touch base and find if the Sheriff's Office had turned up any suspects. Clark came on the line after two rings, and identified himself.

"Detective, it's Harry Caine. I wanted to check in and see how your investigation is going on the Theodore Martin case. Any suspects yet?"

"Oh yeah, Caine. I'm glad you called. We checked you out and it seems you told us a little white lie. I was about to call your hotel. Thanks for saving me the trouble."

"What do you mean I told you a lie?" I said, sounding concerned and a little indignant.

"You can drop the attitude, Caine. We checked with Attorney Nelson and he told us you brought him the signed receipt right after you delivered the packages to Martin Wednesday, just before noon. Why did you go back to Martin's house Thursday morning? It sure as hell wasn't to get a copy of a lost receipt, like you said. Could it be you were returning to the scene of the crime?" Clark's voice was sarcastic.

Silence. I was caught off guard. Nelson never mentioned his being contacted by the Sheriff's Office. I wanted to bring up Gina's murder but thought better of it. Gina's case was in the hands of the Mountain View PD and Clark may not yet be aware that the two murders were probably connected. Not bringing it up would buy me a little more time. At least until he determined that the Mountain View attorney Gina was working for was Nelson. I wasn't going to lie to Clark, but on the other hand I wasn't going to answer questions he didn't ask. In my defense I said, "I was stunned when I went to Martin's house on Thursday. I was there to talk to him about his part in a counterfeit ring and was flabbergasted to find that he had been killed." There, it was out, and I felt ten pounds lighter.

"What in the hell are you talking about, Caine? What counterfeit ring?"

"I was going to tell you everything when I tracked down the source of the paper the money is being printed on."

"Okay, okay. I've heard enough. I want to see you in my office in thirty minutes. Got it?"

"I got it, Detective. Where's your office?"

Sounding irritated, Clark said, "100 block of Main Street in Redwood City. Don't make us come pick you up, Caine."

Things were heating up fast and, if I didn't resolve a few issues quickly, I was going to get burned.

I decided to let Clark know I was hired by Nelson to keep an eye on Martin, and in doing so, discovered his printing operation. I also decided to withhold any further information unless he asked specifically about Gina's murder, which would mean he had made the connection. I pulled into the Sheriff's Office parking lot exactly thirty minutes after speaking with Clark.

Clark was waiting for me in the lobby of the concrete structure. He was showing a serious frown and said in a gruff voice, "Follow me, Caine."

It was an order. I obeyed. We walked the length of a long hallway with a gleaming tile floor and pictures of ex-sheriff's adorning the walls on both sides. I was aware of our footsteps repeatedly being in and then being out of sync. A hell of a thing to notice at a time like this, but it was the kind of thing I always notice. Clark's office door was at the dead-end of the hallway. We entered the office and Clark walked behind his desk and sat down heavily in the high-back, black executive chair. I took a seat on a metal and naugahyde chair directly in front of the desk. I had a feeling of deja vu. It was the same feeling I used to get in high school when I was called into the dean's office for screwing up. Clark looked troubled. He let me take in his look for a long moment and then said, "Tell me why you lied about the reason you were at Martin's house Thursday morning."

Instead of giving Clark an explicit reason why I had lied, I diverted his attention with my story from the time I met Zucker in the boat yard up to the time I saw Martin printing twenty-dollar bills at his place in Mountain View. I was careful to let him know that I had left Martin's house at 3:00 a.m. on Thursday morning believing he was at the house and tucked in for the rest of the night.

Clark appeared to buy my story. He also appeared to have lost his concern over the fact that I had lied about why I was at Martin's house on Thursday morning. Clark said, "I'm going to alert the San Francisco office of the Secret Service, so describe in detail what you saw when you were watching Martin print the money."

I went over the same spiel I had given Nelson on Thursday morning. I provided Clark with all the detail I could recall about the printing operation and the packages of currency paper. I left out the name of Scarapelli Express and its connection to Anthony Falcon in Fernandina Beach. I wanted to pursue that thread without being dogged by Clark or some Secret Service agent, whom I was sure would be all over me immediately after Clark had notified them.

Looking pleased with himself, Clark reported the alleged counterfeiting while I sat in front of his desk listening. He identified me and provided the agent my contact information along with the fact that I was not to leave the area. I wondered how long it would take for the Secret Service to contact Zucker or at least put him under surveillance. After finishing his call, Clark told me that I was to make myself available until he informed me otherwise. He had my number at the hotel and my word that I wouldn't leave the area without his permission until things were cleared up. I hadn't heard any words that made me think I was a prime suspect in either the counterfeiting or the killing of Martin. To my astonishment, Clark didn't mention Gina's murder. I felt sure he was aware of the murder, even though it had occured in another county. The fact that both murders had a connection to Neslon had to surfaced almost immediately. In dealing with law enforcement I found it best not to voluteer information. Things would take their course. It had taken about forty minutes to grind through Clark's questions, and I was feeling a little drained by the time I got back to my car. On the way back to the hotel, I stopped for a burger, onion rings, and a diet soda. I deserved it.

  It was 6:35 p.m. when I reached the hotel. There were five mesages from Nelson. I would call him in the morning. He seemed nervous, and for good cause. I felt like I should dig in and try to find how the paper was moved from ENARC to Fernandina Beach. At the moment I wasn't sure where to start. When in doubt give it the over night treatment. Things usually look clearer in the morning. I put the blackmail videotape in my duffel bag along with Bonnie's telephone records and the report from Kincaid. I watched the local evening news on TV. A short piece was aired regarding Gina's murder. There was no picture of Gina shown, and the information was the same as I had read in the paper.

  It was 9:35 p.m. on the east coast. Too late for business telephone contacts, so I opted for an evening of solitude with a couple glasses of wine and a Ross MacDonald novel from the hotel paperback library. There's nothing like being your own boss.

15

I was up at 8:00 a.m., anxious to find a paper trail that would lead to the currency stock moving from ENARC to Anthony Falcon's Florida Coast Paper. If, in fact, the paper came from ENARC. After breakfast I was back in my room when the desk clerk called to let me know I had received a package. I went to the front desk and picked up a FedEx package sent from New Jersey. It was a copy of the divorce file regarding Zucker v. Zucker. I checked out the transcript and, not to my surprise, found that Zucker Sr. had named Anthony Falcon as the man with whom his wife was having an affair. Bonnie Zucker had confirmed her husband's infidelity charge in order to avoid having Falcon brought into court. The infidelity didn't make the divorce any easier, or more difficult, since no grounds were needed. However, moral, as well as legal issues, can sway judges. There was a statement made by Bonnie that she believed Zucker might physically harm Falcon. It wasn't a big stretch to figure that New Jersey Zucker would have Falcon under his thumb as the price Bonnie and Falcon would pay for not calling it quits before they turned down the covers.

That was all fine and dandy but at the end of the day it was just my word that I had delivered currency paper to Martin. There was no paper to be seen and the receipt I delivered to Nelson only stated that five containers of heirlooms were delivered. I was sure that boat-yard Zucker would stick to that story and even tell the Secret Service the name of the person shipping the heirlooms.

I shuffled through my papers for Bonnie's phone records and found the Fernandina Beach number that appeared ten times in the past two months. I called the number.

An answering machine told me that I had reached the office of Mr. Anthony Falcon and how important my call was to him. It's answering machines that keep genuine insincerity alive and well. I didn't leave a message as requested.

Since Bonnie was talking with Falcon at this number, I assumed Falcon would make calls from this number to his other connections.

I placed a call to an old acquaintance in Tampa who runs a nationwide service called Disconnect America. For sixty dollars, the company would obtain Falcon's last one hundred toll call records or all such records for the past two months, whichever came first. I provided them with Falcon's telephone number, name and address and was told the information would be faxed to me in twenty-four hours. It's a little expensive but what the hell, in for a dime, in for a dollar. I would have the records on Sunday, and by

Monday morning, I should be able to shed some light on the players in Falcon's world.

I had to rethink Nelson's role in this drama after Leon Suggs told me it was Bonnie who provided the info about the currency paper being sent to California. Nelson was looking more like a patsy than a felon. All Nelson needed was to have had Clark, the Secret Service, or the Mountain View PD find Kincaid's video tape hidden in his desk drawer and they would have liked him for blackmailing Martin. If the money printing machines and the currency paper were found, it would be a small jump from blackmailing to counterfeiting and Martin's murder. Feeling a little guilty for leaning too hard on Nelson, I called his office in hopes of clearing the air and letting him know what I had found. I owed him a report since it was his nickel that was keeping me on the case until the end of the day.

Nelson answered on the first ring. Our hellos were a bit awkward. He said, "I tried to reach you all day yesterday, Harry. What have you found since the last time I talked to you. You're on the case until the end of the day today. Right?" He sounded as though he was having an adrenalin rush.

"Yeah, that's right. I've discovered a few things. For starters, I know you didn't have anything to do with any of this criminal activity. I know you won't like hearing this, but it looks as though Bonnie may be the heavy here. She hired a PI to tail Martin long enough to find out he had a sexual hang-up, which she used to blackmail him. The video of Martin engaged in his favorite pastime was hidden in your desk just waiting for the Feds and the local PD to find it and bust you for the counterfeiting and for Martin's murder. Gina learned of the printing machine Martin had invented from listening to conversations in your office.

She passed the information along to her boyfriend. His militia group was getting ready to steal the copying machines and the paper, but they couldn't find them. I don't have a clue where they are either. I found Kincaid's report at Bonnie's house, but I didn't find a gun. I'm not sure who else is involved in this thing. My apologies for thinking you were a bad guy yesterday."

Nelson was silent for a few seconds and then said, "You should have known I wouldn't have anything to do with this mess."

"I can only draw conclusions based on the evidence I find. I want you to know that I haven't told the Sheriff's office anything about Bonnie and no one has asked me about Gina's murder. That's only because they haven't gotten around to me yet. You have any idea where the machines and paper are?"

"Damned if I know. What worries me is what to do about Bonnie. Christ, she practically runs this place by herself. On the other hand, if what you say is true, she should be reported to the Sheriff's Office so they can either confirm her involvement or rule it out. One way or the other. I think I'll close down the office for a week and let things run their course. I'll tell Bonnie I need a break. If she's involve, as you think, either she or Kincaid or both will make a mistake and that'll be the end of that."

Nelson seemed to have easily accepted my conclusions about Bonnie's involvement with the counterfeiting and the murder of Martin. Nelson's attitude surprised me. If asked to bet, I would have put my money on his standing up for her to the bitter end. It would have been a bad bet because he didn't make any attempt to defend her. He gave me the feeling that he hoped Kincaid and Bonnie would take the rap. Maybe I was reading more into it than I should.

Nelson continued, "Can you be in my office in an hour. I have something for you that I'm sure you can use."

"Sure, I'll be there." I hung up and three seconds later my room phone rang. I answered and a deep male voice said, "Caine?"

I said, "Yes."

"Meet me in the lobby... now!"

His accent placed his early development on the streets of New York, or maybe New Jersey. With mild irritation I asked. "Who is this?"

"It doesn't matter. You don't know me and we'll keep it that way. I'll be at your door if you ain't in the lobby in one minute."

"What makes you think I have anything to talk to you about?" He hung up.

I would either have to go out the back way to avoid this guy or go to the lobby - now. If he meant me harm, he wouldn't have called to warn me. I opened my door cautiously and walked to the lobby.

The man standing in front of the clerk's counter by the house telephone was about six foot, two hundred fifty pounds, dark olive complexion and dark short curly hair. He was wearing a wrinkled, brown suit with a brown shirt and a white tie. He could have been a character out of a God Father movie. He looked as though he had been traveling for a while without a chance to clean up. He was soft-spoken when he said, "Caine?"

"Yeah, I'm Caine. What do you want to see me about?"

"I work for a relative of the guy who sent you out here from Daytona Beach. The relative wants to know what happened to the merchandise you delivered. Also, he wants to know what happened to the machines that use this merchandise. Understand?"

I understood. This goon was sent from Zucker Sr. and I didn't want him dogging me. "Have you talked to Bonnie?"

"Yeah. She don't know nothing about where the stuff is. She told us she sent some guy who was working for her, uh, Max Kincaid, to pick up everything from where Martin was doing the printing, but hasn't heard from the fucker since."

I was blown away that Bonnie freely admitted that she had Kincaid take the machines and paper from Martin's PMS store. She's in all the way with the Zuckers and made the mistake of trusting sleaze-ball Kincaid to do her errands. Guys like Kincaid always go into business for themselves whenever the opportunity arises. With a much greater understanding of the situation, I said, "Nelson wanted me to see what I could find about the murder of Theodore Martin. That was before Gina was shot. I guess you know about her?"

"Bonnie told us about her."

"Don't you have a name?"

"You can call me Newark."

"A city for a name. Clever."

"Just tell me what you know wise guy. It has to do with you staying healthy. You know what I mean?"

You bet your ass I knew what he meant. I felt like being cooperative. "Okay, don't get excited. Bonnie hired Max Kincaid to check out Martin and then Martin turns up dead. The machines and paper are gone, and I can only assume they're together, somewhere out there." I said this with a dramatic sweeping gesture, using my arm in a backhand motion.

Newark stared at me. He either didn't get my attempt at levity or he did and was trying to decide on the appropriate punishment. Newark, slow on the comeback, said, "Give me Kincaid's address."

"I can give you his office address. I don't know where he lives."

"I'm warning you, Caine, you should not be doing anything that could be interpreted as being against the interests of the man who sent you here. You should help me find these things I'm looking for or you'll get unhealthy fast."

"Hey, Newark, that's all I know. Let me know if you find the stuff so I can stop worrying about it."

"You'll be the first to know if I find the stuff because we're teaming up for the job. Don't go nowhere, Caine. I'll be in touch very soon."

Newark walked out of the lobby. I watched him go to a white Dodge van and drive away in the direction of Kincaid's office. He probably rented a van in anticipation of finding the machines and paper and was intending to drive them to the east coast.

I didn't like him thinking we were going to be looking for the missing stuff as a team. I'd have to find a way to discourage that idea. Newark gave me the feeing that he would just as soon kill me as look at me, and the feeling made me homesick for my 9mm Glock, stashed in a drawer on the boat.

Newark was knocking on my door fifteen minutes after he left. I walked out of the room and said, "Lets go to the lobby." I didn't want there to be any evidence that this guy was in my room.

"You're going with me, Caine. We're gonna find Kincaid and you better have some ideas where to look."

Feeling a little claustrophobic with Newark tied to me, I said, "I have to meet with Bonnie's boss in a few minutes, and I'll probably get some ideas where Kincaid might be. I'll be back in about an hour. Check in and relax."

"I'm already checked in down the street at the Lazy Six. I'll go with you, Caine."

"Nothing personal, Newark, but I don't think we should be seen together. The Sheriff's department already has their eyes on me and they've alerted the Secret Service to a possible counterfeiting operation. The Sheriff found out that I had delivered containers to Martin the day before he was shot, and I had to tell them that I saw Martin printing money."

"You're not very smart, Caine. Why the fuck did you tell'em anything?"

"I could be wrong but you look like a smart guy and I'm sure that you understand that as a licensed PI in California I'm required to tell the truth to the cops when they ask. I did my job by delivering the packages to Martin and giving the receipt to Nelson. I wasn't told to do anything else and I wasn't told to lie about anything. My job was finished. Nelson hired me to check out Martin for a few days and I took the job because I need the bread. I saw Martin printing the money, and I went to his house Thursday morning to see what he had to say, as part of the work I was doing for Nelson, and he was dead. Cops were all over the place and they asked me what I was doing there. I told them I had lost the receipt Martin had signed for the packages and I was there to get Martin to sign another receipt. The fuzz found out from Nelson that I delivered the receipt to him and braced me about the lie. I had no choice but to tell them why I was in California, who hired me to deliver the packages, and the fact that I had seen Martin printing counterfeit twenties, using the paper I had delivered to him. I can't leave town without permission from the Sheriff's Office. Now does it make sense to you that we shouldn't hang out together?"

"I'm gotta talk to my boss about this, Caine, but I'm telling you, you're gonna help me find this stuff as part of the job Zucker sent you out here to do. Just think of it as a change in the assignment. You find the stuff or say bye-bye to your boat."

Team up with Newark and go to jail for counterfeiting, or lose Newark and lose my boat and who knows what else? I couldn't accept either choice. I would never become a member of a criminal organization, but, for argument's sake, if I did, I sure as hell would not accept being junior to Newark in the scheme of things.

16

Newark reluctantly agreed to meet me in my hotel lobby in one hour. I drove to Nelson's office. His building had a weekend feel. No people and little noises that echoed and seemed louder than usual. Nelson was alone in his office going through some paper work at his desk. I knocked as I opened the door and said, "What's so important? You find something I should know about?"

Nelson looked up without moving his head. He was a picture of the successful lawyer doing some last minute stuff before his Saturday morning tee-off. Christ, do all lawyers play golf? Sounding relaxed, he said, "I thought you should have some protection in case it gets rough out there." Nelson opened his desk drawer, pulled out a small caliber pistol and slid it across a paperless area of his desk.

"Take it. It might come in handy."

"Why the concern?"

"I feel responsible. Is there anything else you found that I ought to know about before you wind up your investigation?"

I was looking at Nelson in a different light. Not one of complicity but one of being a patsy. I no longer felt compelled to hold anything back.

"I know the San Francisco office of the Secret Service was alerted to the counterfeit operation going on somewhere around here. I can't show them any counterfeit currency or printing machines so their interest may not be long lasting. They may even think I'm a nut case. But I expect they'll contact me anytime now. And probably you too. You could have told me that the Sheriff's Office contacted you about my bringing you the receipt for the goods I delivered to Martin. It would have saved me a lot of hassle. Like I told you on the phone, I don't know where the paper or machines are and Zucker's old man sent a goon out here to ride herd on me until I come up with the stuff. He's waiting for me now to go with him to find Max Kincaid. He goes by the name of Newark, and he says Bonnie is helping him. He might also think that maybe she's on your side too. I know you think a lot of her but it looks to me like she's good for Martin's murder and possibly Gina's."

Nelson looked worried and pained before saying, "Hell yes, I think a lot of her. I can't believe she's involved in this thing."

"Get used to the idea, she's involved. I found a video taped to the back of your desk drawer that was obtained by Max Kincaid while he was working for Bonnie. The tape, along with a report was the product of his work. She set you up pal, and you might just as well accept it. She used Kincaid in hopes of getting something on Martin she could use to blackmail him into printing money with his new machine. I'm not sure why she did it, but there is a reason. Count on it."

"What do you mean, the video you found taped to the back of my desk drawer? What the hell have you been up to, Harry? What else do you know about Bonnie that you haven't told me?"

With a grimace I said, "Sorry about the intrusion. I had to check you out after Bonnie told me you hired Kincaid to tail Martin. I talked to Kincaid and he told me you hired him and that he had given you a report with a videotape attached to it. I was looking for the report when I found the videotape in your desk. I figured you were blackmailing Martin. Bonnie was playing you for a sucker and Kincaid was along for the ride."

Nelson hit his desktop with both fists hard enough to shake the hair loose at the front of his head. I got the feeling he was trying to convince me that he was angry. Was I being overly critical? I soothed myself with the knowledge that critical thinking was a mark of intelligence.

"The important thing is you now know I'm not involved in this mess." With a look, Nelson wanted to make sure I agreed with his conclusion. He got an affirmative nod. I was waiting for him to ask me for the tape and the report Kincaid gave to Bonnie, but the demand was not presented and I did not volunteer.

"Thanks for the gun." I picked it up from the desktop and checked the magazine. It was a twenty-five caliber semi-automatic and the clip was missing a few rounds. The chamber was empty and the safety was on. I firmly planted the location and the on-off position of the safety in my mind. Fumbling in the dark for a safety can be lethal. "I'll be in touch. I'm not leaving town for a while and you know where to reach me." Leaving Nelson's office I paused by the fax machine as it was printing a periodic list of the last thirty or so calls. Kincaid's name was at the top of the list. The time of his call was recorded as 10:45 a.m. today. I was driving from my hotel to Nelson's office at that time. I silently repeated the number to myself until reaching the stairs and then jotted it down in my 3x5 notebook. I used the telephone at the corner bookstore to dial the number. The call was answered by an answering machine at Kincaid's office. I hung up immediately, sprinted to my car and drove to Kincaid's office. A light blue older model Thunderbird was parked in the parking slot directly in front of his office door. The rust at the edges of the front fenders and hood, and the filthy condition of the car, was the tip off that it belonged to Kincaid. A man and his car quickly reflect the same degree of grooming.

The hood of the Thunderbird was still warm, and I could see a light in Kincaid's outer office. I tried the door. Locked. I took a credit card from my wallet and slid the lock tongue out of the doorjamb and opened the door. There was no one in the outer office. I called Kincaid's name. No answer. I waited a few seconds listening for sounds of movement in the adjoining office. No sounds. I called again and waited another few seconds before opening the private office door. No sign of Kincaid and nothing in the room but a beat up tan metal desk, a black two-drawer filing cabinet that was as empty as the desk, a black, mostly plastic, desk chair, and a brown wood guest chair. The office furniture ensemble could have won the worst in show at any furniture market. It looked as though Kincaid took his treasures and split. I picked up his phone and dialed *69. A female voice answered the phone.

"You've reached Peninsula Auto Rentals. May I help you?"

Running on autopilot I said, "Yeah, I'm checking to see if Mr. Kincaid has picked up his rental yet."

"Who's calling please?"

"This is his field manager, Vic Slanner. I was trying to figure when he would arrive. By the way, what did you have available for him?" I'd used the name Vic Slanner in pretext calls so many times he almost seemed real.

"Oh, he was quite pleased with the new Ford cargo van. After all it only has a few miles on it. Who wouldn't be pleased."

"Exactly. Did Mr. Kincaid tell you if he or someone else would be retuning the vehicle to your lot?"

"Our records show Mr. Kincaid returning the van to our lot in Carmel tomorrow morning. When we picked him up at his office we offered to let him keep it until Monday morning at a very small additional charge, but he chose to return it tomorrow morning in Carmel. Anyway, you won't have to drive it back to us."

"Great. You made my day, and the little lady's day as well. That gives us the whole weekend off. We'll definitely use your services the next time out. Oh, by the way, I need to make a note of the tag number for our records. Mr. Kincaid never covers those little details."

"Just a minute I'll look it up."

She sounded as though I was beginning to wear her out. It only took a few seconds for her to read off the tag number of the van. She muttered some kind of happy ending words, I said thanks and hung up.

Where was Kincaid going? Why is he returning the van to Carmel? If I were going to return a rental car to Carmel in the morning it would be because I would already be in Carmel. I wouldn't drive from somewhere else to Carmel for that reason. If I had to drive I would just return the car to Mountain View. Kincaid's car was parked at his office, so how was he going to get back here. He could be meeting someone in Carmel or he could be using Carmel as a low profile point of departure if he needed to leave the area without drawing attention to himself. My best bet would be to wait for him at the Peninsula Auto Rentals lot in Carmel early tomorrow morning. I hadn't decided whether I would confront him at the rental lot or just follow him. With that semi-baked plan in mind, I headed back to the hotel to meet Newark before he got overheated about me being a little late.

Newark was sitting in his white Dodge van near the front door of the hotel when I pulled into the parking lot. His jaw tightened when he saw me. He threw open the van door, slid out of the driver's seat onto the black top and started toward me. His looks hadn't changed. He could have used the hour and a half to take a little rest and clean up.

"Where the hell have you been, Caine? You almost made the mistake of your life because I was about to come after you."

"Where would you have started to look, Newark?"

Looking confused, Newark said, "Don't worry about that. I would have found you." Newark stared into space with his mouth hanging open as though he were trying to recall something. He probably had the resources to help him find people in Newark, but he looked like it just dawned on him that he had no resources in Northern California.

In a conspiratorial manner I said, "I told you I'd probably get an idea where we could find Kincaid after talking to Nelson. Well, I've got two hot leads. One is north of here and the other is south. He is either hold up in an apartment in Tiburon or at a friend's house in Carmel. I have the addresses of both places and in the interest of finding this guy fast, I think we ought to split up and cover both places at once. Time is of the essence here, Newark. What do you think?"

I took out my pocket notebook, wrote down an address in Tiburon, tore out the page, and handed it to Newark. I remembered the name of the street in Tiburon from casework some years ago. It was a convincing story and I could see by the look on Newark's face that he was cranking my info through his carbon computer. I was waiting for him to ask me where I got the addresses. I had a story in place to cover it.

Five seconds passed before Newark got a penetrating look in his eyes and said, "How'd you find out that he was at one of these places?"

"According to Nelson, Bonnie told him that she wouldn't be in for a few days and Nelson decided to close his office for a week. She left a message on Nelson's answering machine that she could be reached at one of two telephone numbers. It's a no-brainer that she'll go where Kincaid is. I ran a cross directory on the numbers and got the addresses. Neither number answers when you call, but that's par for the course. They probably have a ring code set up to filter out all calls but their own."

Newark bought it. In his manner of taking control, he directed me to go to the Carmel address and he would take Tiburon since he knew where it was in relation to San Francisco. Even though I was prepared to supply one, Newark didn't ask for the Carmel address. I was saved the effort to convince him that I should take Carmel. I must be living right.

Newark became animated, and said, "Let's go, Caine. The boss is waitin' to hear from me and I need to have good news for him. I've got my cell phone and I want you to call me from Carmel just before you go to the house. Understand?"

Newark verbally gave me his cell number, which I recorded in my pocket notebook. Falling right into step I pledged my wholehearted support and suggested we hit the road.

"Okay, Caine. Remember, I know you ain't leaving town soon, and if you try to ditch me it'll be your ass because you're easy to find."

"Don't sweat it, Newark, I want to find the stuff as much as you do." I didn't complete the sentence, which would have been, 'but for totally different reasons.'

"Don't you think you should know what Kincaid looks like before going out after him?"

Newark's face affected a momentary blank stare before his expression turned to one of irritation. He said, "What do you think I was about to ask you, smart guy?"

I visualized my only meeting with Kincaid and described him to Newark, whose comment was, "He sounds like a pretty relaxed guy to me, Caine. You think he'll be packing heat?"

In hopes of ending the conversation, I turned to walk toward the hotel entrance and said over my shoulder, "Wouldn't you?"

17

The ride to Carmel was a tonic. The heavy weekday traffic was absent and the weather made me feel alive. Sixty-two degrees and a bright blue sky contrasting the green Santa Cruz Mountains that separate Silicon Valley from the coast. There's something about the California coast that gives me a sense of excitement and personal freedom. Maybe it's seeing the mountains and the ocean cliffs in one big panoramic view that does it. I've never been able to figure it out, but it's there. I made my way south along the rim of Monterey Bay past the army base at Fort Ord, in and out of the towns of Sand City, Seaside, Monterey, Pacific Grove and into Carmel. The ride from Mountain View to Carmel took about ninety minutes and I felt refreshed when I arrived. I'm a sucker for beautiful scenery.

Carmel consists mostly of high priced homes and high rents for high priced homes. The downtown business section is full of boutiques, small upscale restaurants, and bed and breakfast inns. In the older section of town, a large number of houses have no numbered addresses. A typical address in those days might have been, person's name, middle of the block of Santa Fe Street between 8th and 9th. Because of the variety of addressing schemes everyone had to go to the post office to pick up their mail. It was a daily social event.

Peninsula Auto Rentals' lot in Carmel was a block off the main drag, called Ocean Avenue, near the Pacific Coast Highway. I checked into the Downtown Motel two blocks from the car lot after looking around the area for the white Ford cargo van.

I called Newark. I had to put closure to the scam that sent him to Tiburon and me to Carmel. He answered so fast he must have been holding the phone waiting for my call. "It's Caine. I checked the house. Kincaid isn't there. How'd you make out with the Tiburon address?"

Newark was silent for a few seconds, and then said, "That address you gave me was an apartment complex and there's no way I could tie Kincaid to any of the apartment numbers. The manager never heard of Kincaid and didn't recall anyone matching his description. Don't try to pull a fast one on me, Caine. I'm no fool. You screw around with me on this thing and you've lost your boat. I'm not going to tell you again. Next time I'll call Zucker, and your boat's gone."

"Sometimes leads don't turn out to be much of anything, but you still have to follow through on them. You ought to know that, Newark."

While he was thinking that over I slipped in the story of why I would not be back at the hotel today, by saying,

"I hope this won't bother you too much, Newark, but I won't be coming back to the hotel tonight. I'm going to spend the night at my sister's house in Santa Cruz. I'll be back by noon tomorrow."

"You better be. Or else!"

"Don't sweat it, Newark. I'll be there like I said. Don't you trust anyone?"

I was relieved to get goon face off my back temporarily, even though I would have to encounter him tomorrow. I decided I would drive around the area's main roads and check the hotels, motels and B&B's for the white Ford Cargo Van. I knew it was like looking for a needle in a haystack and I had told myself earlier that it would be a waste of time, but I couldn't resist. Most people would just call it quits. Me, I like to go for the long shot when there is little down side to losing. Maybe that's why I'm at my particular station in life.

It was 8:00 p.m. when I told myself I had covered all the bases. I drove back to the Downtown Motel to clean up before going out to eat.

I found a small restaurant on Mission Street called Kathy's Grill. It was the kind of place where eating alone wasn't a conspicuous act. There were three singles having dinner when I walked inside. The lighting was brighter than in the more expensive joints but the food was just right. Pork chops, applesauce, green beans, and iced tea. The meal was listed on the menu as 'Gringo's Delight'. Suits me.

As it turned out, the main attraction at Kathy's Grill was not the food, but the restaurant's owner, Anne Mitchell. We made eye contact the moment I walked into the place. She looked to be in her mid-thirties, five eight, dark brown hair and a figure she couldn't, and shouldn't, hide behind her loose fitting sweater and full skirt. Her square jaw gave her a determined look. Her bright brown eyes looked into my soul. She moved around the restaurant with the grace and confidence of a woman who knew exactly what she was doing and why she was doing it. After we had several short verbal exchanges when she passed my table, I invited her to join me for coffee. She sat down and said, "I'm Anne Mitchell and I hope you're enjoying my restaurant."

We made small talk for a short time. She seemed to keep up a barrier until the conversation got around to her owning the restaurant and how long she had owned it. She appeared to relax when she began talking about herself. She told me she bought the restaurant a year ago and is now considering buying a house in Carmel. Wanting me to carry the conversation she said, "What do you do for a living?"

"I don't usually like to say what I do but you have a quality about you that makes it easy to tell it like it is. I'm a private investigator and I'm down here from Mountain View working on a case. I'm leaving in the morning, and I'll probably leave California in a few days to go back to Daytona Beach."

That established the length of time I could be involved with her. I noticed a flicker of calculation in her eyes before she said, "Do you have business in Daytona Beach or do you live there?"

"My boat is there and I live on my boat. It's a long story. I was on my way to do some island living when, as fortune would have it, I needed to make some money and the case I'm on now dropped into my lap."

"Where were you on the way from and who with?" Now she was getting to it. Is there a wife, or girl friend back in Daytona Beach? I liked her directness. I said, "I was coming from Washington, D.C. I built my boat there while working for the Feds. When I finished the boat, I said good-bye to all my land locked attachments and came south, by myself."

A brief memory of those land locked attachments flashed across my mind. Two affairs that made for great memories but no permanent connections. I didn't verbalize the thought. She smiled warmly. I wondered if she was pleased at the fact that I wouldn't be around very long or the fact that I currently had no female attachments. Both pieces of information could be important to her for several reasons. One; I was the perfect guy for a one-night stand or two; I would be an interesting long-term relationship. I was betting on number one. The prospect was warming.

"What about you? What brought you here?" I said with sincere interest. Locking me in her gaze she said, "I was married for a couple of years and it didn't work out. It was in San Jose. I always liked coming to Carmel and when I saw this restaurant listed for sale in the paper, I used part of my settlement money to buy it. Like I said, I'm looking around for a house to buy and might buy the place I'm leasing. Not sure yet." She put her hand on my thigh and said, "It's almost closing time. I'll have Jenny close up for me tonight and we'll go check out the hot spots. That shouldn't take long in Carmel. You up for it?"

This lady didn't waste time. I smiled and said, "I sure am." She didn't know I was speaking somewhat literally.

"I have to go put a few things away. I'll be right back."

I could feel the warmth of her hand leave my thigh. She probably felt the warmth of my thigh leave her hand. She returned in a few minutes and I followed her white Mercedes to her house, a few blocks south of Ocean Avenue. The house looked like a Frank Lloyd Wright student designed it. It blended in with the trees and contours of the surrounding ground like it grew out of it. Wright called it organic architecture. A gated courtyard separated the front door of the house from the street. The gate was heavy wrought iron and the tip of each vertical bar was painted gold giving the appearance of being covered with gold leaf. The double car driveway was long and led to a garage that didn't match the house. I thought the garage was an example of inorganic architecture. Anne parked her car deep into the driveway near the front of the garage. She motioned with her index finger that she would be with me in one minute. She disappeared into the house.

    When she returned she was wearing a straight black dress with spaghetti straps, carrying a small purse in one hand, and a light-weight jacket in the other. The dress was cut low enough so that the sensuous upper curves of her breasts were visible. I imagined the lower portion. Bending forward to get into the car she exhibited a full frontal invitation. It was beautiful. Her eyes and lips smiled when she looked up at me to make sure I enjoyed the scenery. I did. She had rolled out the red carpet. After getting her seat belt on, Anne said, "Where are we going, Harry?"

    "I'd like to find a quiet, semi-dark lounge that plays jazz. And by jazz, I mean cool, quiet jazz. I don't mean to be a snob about it, but to sum it up there are two kinds of music. Music I like and music I don't like. How about you?"

    Anne was thoughtful and remained silent for a few seconds before saying, "I know the kind of jazz your talking about and it brings back memories. My brother was an aspiring jazz musician in high school. He listened to everything Plas Johnson recorded with Henry Mancini and tried to imitate his style. But it didn't work out. My father was a professional jazz musician. Played all the reed instruments. He even did a stint with Basie and Maynard Ferguson's big band. He finally settled into the hotel lounge scene in San Francisco for the rest of his career. He's retired now and still lives in San Francisco. I've always been proud of his accomplishments. My brother, on the other hand, became an engineer and I married an engineer who became a Silicon Valley big shot. Anyway, I have a place in my heart for the kind of jazz you've described."

She said the right thing. The woman was beautiful and we shared a like for the same kind of music. I was hooked. I said, "Since we both understand what we mean by jazz, where does one go around here to hear it?"

"The most popular place is the Hog's Head Inn. The place always has a small group playing our kind of music. It's about the only consistent venue for jazz in Carmel, and one of the few places that stay open late."

"Show me the way, lady."

Anne happily directed me to the Hog's Head Inn. We had a few drinks, listened to some of the best live jazz I had heard in years and talked non-stop after listening intently to the first few tunes. Without any detail, I told her I was involved in trying to resolve a counterfeiting case. Her interest was piqued when I said the word, "counterfeiting."

It was obvious she had some knowledge of the subject. "I saw a documentary on public television about the Treasury Department and the Secret Service's effort to make currency more counterfeit resistant. A segment of the program was dedicated to identifying organized distribution networks and finding how the fake money is concealed and shipped from place to place. I was surprised to learn that Colombia and Bulgaria are the prime producers of counterfeit $100 bills on the international scene. They also said that fake U.S. currency produced in Colombia and Bulgaria account for almost half of all counterfeits successfully passed in the United States. Apparently China is a distribution point for counterfeit bills but doesn't produce them."

I was impressed. I guessed that her interest in counterfeiting came from the fact that restaurants are targets for passing bogus money. I could tell she wasn't going to have to eat any fake dough at her restaurant.

I mostly kept quiet and listened while she told me some of her likes and dislikes. She disliked cold coffee, people who can't get to the point, ostentatious displays of wealth, and liars. The dislike of ostentatious displays of wealth didn't quite jibe with her house and the Mercedes, but I let it slide. It's scary how fast I can lower the bar for the possibility of sex. She loved quiet weekends at the beach, reading Ross MacDonald and John D. Macdonald mysteries, watching Jodi Foster and Gene Hackman movies, and eating steak and salad. All in all, my kind of woman.

We got back to her house at 1:00 a.m. She invited me in. I accepted. The rest of the night was like something out of the sweetest dream I've ever had, but it wasn't a dream. The beauty of her soft, smooth skin, trim body and warm personality made me want to stay with this magnificent woman forever. We promised to stay in touch, but in reality the obstacles of my involvment with Nelson, and her managing a restaurant in Carmel made the possibility remote. Our night together could be one of those turning points in life. A little time would tell.

Our passion subsided into blissful contentment at 2:30 a.m. I had just enough energy and focus left, before falling asleep, to set her clock alarm for 5:00 a.m.

18

My biological clock woke me minutes before the alarm went off. I shut it off before it could wake Anne, and quietly got dressed. I left a note in the kitchen giving her my telephone number at the hotel in Mountain View. I also wrote the name of my boat and number of the Daytona Beach Boat Yard. I left the house making sure the door was locked. I wanted to see her again before leaving for Florida. If I didn't, I would contact her when I moved my boat. Our fast track romance happened because I had to leave the area, and I wondered how it would have gone had I lived close enough to see her regularly. I had no regrets. The thought that I would be connected to her at some level for a long time was stimulating.

I drove back to the Downtown Motel where I had paid for a room that I didn't use, at least not to sleep in. I showered, shaved, and put on a clean shirt, a pair of khakis and my sport jacket. I looked like a professional whose work takes place out of the office. Being out of the office was an initial reason I was attracted to being a private investigator. For me, offices are synonymous with claustrophobia.

It was 5:45 a.m. when I checked out of the motel. The Peninsula Rental lot was two blocks away. Too far to see from the motel. I drove the car to a spot across the street from Peninsula Rentals' lot. It was a warehouse; the kind of place where a parked car looks anonymous. I had the forethought to bring along a book I borrowed from my Mountain View hotel. Read a paragraph, look up, read a paragraph, look up. I continued the process for three hours before Kincaid showed up in the white Ford cargo van. An employee of the rental car company had just taken down the chain that hung across the driveway entrance and opened the door to the little shack sitting in the center of the lot.

Kincaid got out of the van and walked into the office with papers in hand. In a moment, the car lot employee and Kincaid emerged from the office and walked to the van. The employee circled the van checking for dings. He opened the two back doors and I could see into the van. It was empty. He closed the back doors and handed Kincaid the clipboard. Kincaid wrote something and handed the clipboard back. The employee removed the sheet he was writing on and handed him a copy that he folded and shoved into his pocket. Kincaid walked quickly to a waiting cab that had arrived at the car lot five seconds behind him. It was show time. The cab pulled onto the street heading toward the Downtown Motel. I started my car and pulled out behind them, leaving enough room between us to look inconspicuous. I had no idea where Kincaid was going. If I lost him there would be no way to intercept him again. Kincaid was the only connection I had to the machines and paper. Losing him was not an option.

The cab went south to Ocean Avenue and then north on Highway 1. I followed a quarter of a mile back until I saw it turn off at Freemont Street in Monterey. I sped up and closed the gap, catching the cab just as it started through the intersection after stopping at a red light. There were two cars between the cab and me, making the tail a little more comfortable. The cab turned onto highway 68 going toward Salinas. A mile down the road the cab turned onto Olmstead Road. A sign with an arrow stated that the Monterey airport was straight ahead.

It was a small airport. I could see the air control tower and the runways, which looked long enough to handle large commercial passenger jets. There were a large number of small private planes sitting at their tie downs along the way to the passenger terminal building. Several private jets were parked near the terminal building.

One of them was standing ready with the passenger door open and what looked to be a pilot stationed at the foot of the stairs leading into the plane. Kincaid hopped out of the cab at the front of the terminal, paid the driver and quickly moved inside.

I parked at the first empty spot nearest the terminal entrance and jogged into the building. Kincaid was at the far end of the terminal talking with the person behind the counter at the luggage and freight loading area. He was showing a piece of paper to an employee who nodded his head. The employee picked up a telephone, said a few words and hung up. Thirty seconds later a double door opened and a luggage tram drove into the area.

Then I saw the two boxes with their cables tied to their sides with heavy duct tape, and the containers of paper that I had delivered to Martin. The driver and the attendant hoisted the two metal boxes onto the tram, followed by the five containers of paper. One of the containers had been opened.

The tram left the building and I quickly moved to a window to get a view of it moving out of the terminal building. The tram drove directly to the waiting private jet with the open door and the pilot standing at the bottom of the stairs. The pilot and the tram driver loaded the metal boxes into the plane through the passenger door. The five containers of paper followed.

I saw Kincaid walk from the terminal building to the private jet dressed in his sweatshirt, jeans and tennis shoes. He was carrying a small overnight bag. It was decision time. I could try to stop the plane. Or, I could record the identification numbers on the plane's tail and determine its destination through the flight plan filed with the FAA. I could get killed if I physically tried to stop the plane, and there was the extreme likelihood that no body would believe me when I told them what the plane was carrying, in order to get them to stop the take-off.

I took my note pad from my coat pocket and recorded the tail numbers of the plane. The pilot boarded, pulled the door closed and taxied for take-off.

I found the office of the Director of Airport Operations and requested the destination of the plane whose tail number was 155286N. In hopes of lighting a fire under him, I showed him my California PI license and said, "The plane is carrying an entire counterfeiting operation on board along with the guy who owns it. I'm going to notify the Secret Service so they can intercept it."

I gave him more information that he needed, especially since the flight plan is public information. The operations manager stared blankly at me for a moment, seemingly unimpressed, and then said, "That's an FAA matter. They are the only ones who can tell you where that plane is going. You'll have to call them. The FAA guys are over there in the control tower." The manager pointed in the direction of the control tower.

"Can I go into the control tower?"

"No, you'll have to call them. Here's the number." The manager wrote the number on a scrap piece of paper and handed it to me.

I went to a public phone and placed a call to the FAA number. A man answered and let me know he was the FAA station manager. I gave him the tail number of the Lear jet and asked him to give me the planes destination. He said he could do that and put me on hold. The phone was silent for about two minutes. Just when I was beginning to think I had been abandoned, the station manager returned to the phone.

"It's going to make a stop in San Diego before going on to its final destination, which is Bogotá, Colombia."

"Thanks, you've just contributed to a sounder economy." I hung up and fished some quarters out of my pocket. In the remote chance of finding Detective Clark at work on a Sunday, I called his number at the San Mateo County Sheriff's Office. He answered immediately.

"Detective Clark, It's Harry Caine. I'm in Monterey and to make a long story short, I found the counterfeiting machines, the paper that goes with them, and Max Kincaid, the guy who presently has possession of the stuff."

Clark, with more than a hint of scarcasm said, "You didn't find who shot Martin?"

Our exchange was not starting out as I expected. I said, "I haven't been in contact with the Secret Service, and I figured that since you've already talked with them, you would want to tell them where they could find the stuff I claimed to have seen."

"Okay, Caine, lets hear it." Heavy sigh.

"They just took off in a private jet from the Monterey airport. The number of the plane is 155286N. I was hoping you could get the Secret Service guys to intercept it and grab Max Kincaid at the same time. According to the flight plan, the plane is stopping in San Diego, and then on to Bogotá, Colombia. In case you aren't aware of it, Colombia produces about half of the counterfeit one hundred dollar banknotes that get passed each year in the U.S." Knowledge is power. I continued, "I think Kincaid is involved with the murder of Theodore Martin and possibly that of Gina Wilson, in case you haven't connected the two killings. He was taking orders from Bonnie Bliss and she's up to her neck in this thing."

With another heavy sigh, Clark said, "Okay, Caine. I'll notify the Secret Service and you'd better be right. I don't like looking like a fool. You be in my office tomorrow morning. We need to go over this whole thing again. Got it? And by the way, Caine, you must think we're totally stupid. We know the Gina Wilson murder is connected to the Martin murder and understand that attorney Nelson is the link between the two, even though the Wilson murder is being investigated by the Mountain View PD. Does that surprise you?"

I said, "Hey, I'm just trying to help. I'll be there by 10:00 a.m."

With that comment, Clark hung up. I was beginning to develop a higher opinion of Clark, even though he didn't trust me, all because of one little white lie. You'd think he'd have a clearer understanding of human nature, considering his position.

I stopped for breakfast in Seaside, and scoffed down some bacon and eggs. I got back to my hotel in Mountain View very close to 12:00 p.m. Guess who was waiting for me.

Newark was sitting in his van in front of the entrance to the hotel. He got out of the van and walked to my car, scowling. I guessed he was under a lot of pressure from Zucker to find the machines and paper. It's likely that he had to make good or else. He was practically foaming at the mouth when he reached my car, at the same time I opened the door to get out.

"You're cutting it a little close, Caine. In another minute or two I would have been after your ass." Newark said it with enough tension in his voice that I thought he was going to explode.

"I told you I'd be back at noon, and its noon. Do I keep my word, or what?"

"Yeah, I'm real impressed. I've got to find that stuff today or my neck's in a noose. And since you're supposed to help me, your neck'll be in a noose too. Know what I'm saying?" Both of Newark's fists clinched as he made the statement. He was wound up tighter than a bull's ass at fly time. He sounded desperate, and I had no doubt that he was behind the eight ball with his boss.

"Jesus, you being so up-tight inhibits my thinking process. I want to find the stuff too. We're going to find it, but its not going to jump into our lap. I'll go with you for the sake of getting my boat back but my heart is definitely not in it. As far as Zucker is concerned, I was hired to deliver the containers, get a receipt for the delivery and give the receipt to Nelson. I did my job. Why the hell is

Zucker forcing me to find the machines and paper? I didn't have anything to do with them being stolen. Damn!"

I let it sink in for a moment and followed up with, "My gut feeling is that Bonnie may have more information than she's giving you. Why don't you go see her at her house and probe a little deeper. You're probably not aware of it, but her loyalty is to her son, not to your boss. Who knows what she'll do to help her son. See what I mean, Newark? Think how you'd look to your boss if you, not me, figured it out that Bonnie is putting the screws to you guys so the whole operation belongs to her son. Like I said, I believe Bonnie is holding out on you. Think about it while I pick up my mail and go to my room to clean up a little. I'll be back in five minutes."

I was grasping at straws, but I couldn't come up with anything else at the moment that had the possibility of getting Newark off my back. I walked into the lobby. The desk clerk motioned to me. I felt like I was becoming a permanent resident at the hotel. I told myself to talk to Nelson about the bill. Hopefully I could just charge it to his credit card. I saw the clerk reach into the box with my room number on it and pull out a thin packet of paper.

"This came for you this morning, Mr. Caine."

"Thanks. Have I had any calls?"

"I'll check." The desk clerk went to the switchboard and shuffled through a short stack of messages.

I had one. I had been wondering when I would be summoned by the Treasury Department and wouldn't you know it, the message was from one John Lewis of the U.S. Treasury Department. Oh boy, here it comes. There was a number written on the paper and a one liner above the caller's name that said 'call when you get in.' I needed to make that call, but first I needed to look at the packet of information that arrived this morning containing the recent cell phone records for Anthony Falcon. If I looked at them in the presence of Newark he might be able to figure out that I was trying to find a connection between Falcon and someone at ENARC in Massachusetts. It wasn't likely, but I didn't want to take the chance. I walked back to the lobby and found Newark pacing in front of the main desk.

Before I could say anything he blurted out his plan, "I've been thinking, Caine. You may have something about Bonnie, and I appreciate your concern for me making good with my boss. So I think the best thing to do is for me to go find Bonnie and have a talk with her. And it's best I do that alone so she won't get back to my boss and tell him it was your idea to question her. You wait here and I'll get back to you if I need your help."

Child psychology worked beautifully on Newark. Probably the only reason Zucker, Sr. had him around. In a slightly disappointed tone I said, "Well, if you think it's best. I'll wait here to hear how it went." Newark left the lobby walking like a man in control of his destiny.

19

John Lewis' interest was in the federal matter of counterfeiting, not the State matter of Martin and Gina's murder. Falcon's phone records could provide a significant piece of evidence, if I could tie him to an ENARC employee.

I opened the package and found that Falcon's phone records for the past two months contained 52 calls. With records in hand, I went to the lobby and sat down at their newly installed Internet-connected guest computer. Some Internet home pages have a connection to the white pages, yellow pages, and maps. This one did not. I typed in the name of 'Google.com', a good first attempt Internet search program, and depressed the return key. Google immediately prompted me to type in what it was I wanted to find. I typed in two words: ENARC Company. Up popped the address and telephone number for ENARC. The company was in Dalton, Massachusetts, and had an area code of 413. Twelve calls on Falcon's phone records were prefixed with the area code of 413. Seven of those were to the same 413 number in Pittsfield, Massachusetts. With a little digging, I found the Pittsfield number belonged to a Michael Lawrence. The other five calls were to an unlisted number that matched ENARC's number except for the last three digits. My heart sped up a bit. The last three digits could be an extension to ENARC's main number. Extension numbers are never listed. I called the unlisted number and was greeted by a female voice that announced I had reached the shipping department of ENARC.

With a surprised sound in my voice I asked, "Is this the ENARC Company?"

"It certainly is. How may I help you?"

Hoping that ENARC was a 24/7 operation that staffed all their departments with a nominal duty person during the second and third shifts, I asked, "Is there a Human Resources person on duty today? I need to verify a current employment."

"One moment, sir."

Another female voice answered. "Human Resources. This is Renee. How may I help you?"

"I'm with Sundown National Bank Credit Card Department. I need to verify the current employment of a Michael Lawrence."

"We can only provide the date of hire on a current employee."

"That's all I need. I don't have a middle initial and his date of birth and social security number are illegible. They send these applications down to me thinking I can work some kind of magic. Can you believe, I have to try to resolve some of these applications on a Sunday? I told 'em

I'd try to verify his employment with just the name. Is it possible?"

"I think we can find him by name only. Hold on sir." About ten seconds went by and the female voice reappeared. "This must be him. It's the only Michael Lawrence employed at ENARC. You got lucky. His hire date is 10-31-93."

"Could you tell me his department, or his job title?"

"Well, if you had a department listed on his application I could tell you if he is still in that department. But nothing else."

The number on Falcon's phone records went to the shipping department so I said, "It looks like Shipping Department, but it's so blurred I'm not sure."

"Yes, he is currently employed in the shipping department. That help?"

"Yeah, thanks, you've been a big help. I'll get a gold star from my boss for being able to process this one on a Sunday. Thanks again."

I'd give five-to-one odds that Michael Lawrence was the ENARC mole. Lewis could figure it out from here.

Lewis answered the phone with 'hello', and identified himself at my request, after I identified myself. In my most cooperative voice, I said, "I just got your message, Agent Lewis. I assume you called as a result of Detective Clark's information regarding the counterfeiting operation I've seen."

Lewis had a tenor voice with an edge. He said, "Your assumption is correct. Are you available for a face-to-face in the next half hour or so?"

"Sure. Name the place."

"I just finished talking with Detective Clark and I can be at your place in twenty minutes. Clark said you're staying at the California Hotel on El Camino in Palo Alto. Is that still correct?"

"Yeah, that's correct. I'll be waiting for you in the lobby."

"Fine. I'll see you then."

I hung up and mentally reviewed the sequence of events leading up to the discovery of Martin printing the money and seeing the machines and paper taking off in the Lear jet from Monterey. I was uptight about being questioned by a Secret Service agent. Maybe it was their reputation of being hard-nosed. Or, maybe it was because I felt guilty about carrying the currency paper to Martin. Self-analysis is not my strong suit. I didn't like the unfocusing effect it had on me. To remove the yoke of further moral implications, I told myself that my impending dealings with the Secret Service would boil down to one fact. I had some information and they would either act on it or file it. Very simple. No big deal. I'm not the bad guy here, just a little late in speaking up.

John Lewis walked into the lobby in a manner that announced to the world that he had arrived, and that you had better pay attention to him. He was about thirty, short, thin, wore sun glasses, a dark suit, a crisp white shirt, a blue and white checkered tie, and shiny black shoes with thick soft soles that were meant for walking. He stopped just inside the door, looked around, and spotted me sitting in an over stuffed chair at the far end of the lobby near the Internet computer. I made no move or gesture of recognition as he approached. It's my way of gaining some control. When he was ten feet from me and still in stride, he asked in a voice that sounded like a boy trying to sound like a man, "Are you Harry Caine?"

Without moving to get up or extend my hand, I said, "That's me. Who are you?" As if I didn't know.

"I'm Agent Lewis, Secret Service. We spoke about twenty minutes ago." Lewis removed his bi-fold ID wallet from his inside coat pocket and flipped it open showing an ID card and a badge. With his other hand he offered me his business card in a manner that said I should take it.

I nodded in acceptance and said, "Yeah, well have a seat and let's talk."

Lewis backed into the chair opposite me and sat down, making sure he didn't wrinkle the crease in his pants. He said, "Okay, Harry. Deputy Clark tells me you witnessed the printing of some counterfeit money. That tends to get us excited. You want to tell me about it?" He came off as patronizing. He used an open-ended question so I could start wherever I wanted and step into any hole I cared to make for myself.

I immediately didn't like him using my first name when he referred to himself as Agent Lewis and not John Lewis. So, to keep things on an even keel, and before answering his question, I said, "What's your first name, Agent Lewis?"

"I don't go by my first name. It's Agent Lewis."

"I don't go by mine either. It's Mr. Caine."

Lewis got the message and it made our relationship clear. Equals. It's all part of the control game. He took notes while I unloaded my story on him from the first meeting with Zucker in the boat yard to seeing the Lear jet take off in Monterey. I didn't have to refer to notes to recall the tail number of the plane. Impressive, I thought. His heavy note taking strengthened my long-standing resolve to take interview notes only when absolutely necessary. It's distracting. I was kind enough not to mention it to him. Lewis was especially interested in the connection between Anthony Falcon and Michael Lawrence. He asked me twice how I determined that Lawrence was Falcon's contact at ENARC.

Lewis put down his notebook and gave me a stern look. He asked, "When were you planning to give us the information about the counterfeiting operation? From what you tell me, I assume that if the murder of Theodore Martin had not occurred you would not have told anyone about the counterfeiting. Or were you waiting for the right time so you could look like a hero? Is it possible that you were complicit in the counterfeiting operation and things went bad for you so you flipped on your buddies? After all, you lied to Detective Clark about why you returned to Martin's house on the morning he was shot. Why should I believe otherwise?"

Was that lie destined to haunt me forever? Since I admitted to carrying the currency paper to Palo Alto, I guessed Lewis could make a pretty strong case for me being involved up to my neck, depending on how much he needed to come up with a perp. In my own defense, I said, "Do you think I would have told Clark my story if I were a player in this thing? I was trying to figure it all out and then I was going to give my evidence to Clark. I'll admit I may have been a little over zealous. I've been out of the business for a couple of years and I was excited about solving a case whose tentacles reached from coast to coast. Can you blame me?"

"Actually, I can. I'm sure your license with the state of California requires you to report any crime that you witness or have knowledge of. I've got a lot of leverage here, and I'm going to hold it over you until I sort things out. Clark tells me you're not permitted to leave the area without his approval. Is that correct?"

This little pompous prick was really irritating me. The irritation came from the fact that he was right. I said, "Yeah, so don't sweat me leaving. I'm still retained by my client to investigate the murders of Martin and Wilson. I've told you everything I know about the counterfeiting operation, and just so we're clear, my motivation for telling you was not to save my ass. I'm being a law-abiding citizen here, which I hope you recognize. Don't you think you ought to be notifying your San Diego guys to meet that plane?"

"I know what I ought to be doing, Caine. For your information my guys are already on it. You watch what you do from here on in, because we'll be looking at you."

That told me he wasn't going to push the idea of me being criminally involved, and I felt free to say, "That's Mr. Caine."

Lewis ignored my comment, took out his notebook again and reviewed his writing before asking,

"Where did you get Falcon's phone records?"

"I have a friend in the business, and I never divulge a source. How about you?"

With that Lewis closed his notebook, stood up and said in an official tone, "We'll be in touch, Caine. Make yourself available."

It was reasonable speculation on my part that Lawrence had something to do with getting the paper out of the ENARC plant, and I knew Lewis would follow up on it. Lewis was a pompous ass, but a detail guy who knew how to organize information. That's a prime prerequisite to being a successful investigator.

I was now a blip on the Secret Service's radar screen. I felt an urge to get back to my boat.

20

I was anxious to finish my involvement with Nelson, the Sheriff's office and the Secret Service. It was a no-brainer that the Sheriff's office would allow me to leave town if I turned over evidence that pointed to the identity of the killer or killers. Even though I thought Bonnie, or Max Kincaid did the killings, I had no hard evidence to offer and the Sheriff's office would care less about what I thought. No weapon had been found, at least to my knowledge, and, at the moment, I'd lost track of Bonnie and Newark. I thought Kincaid might now be in the hands of the Secret Service. A sick feeling in the pit of my stomach told me I'd better find all three of them. If one or more of those three were directly involved with the killings, I would be persona-non-grata. The last thing any of them would want is for me to be able to testify to what I'd seen and found out.

I left the hotel and drove to Bonnie's house. On the way I reached into my duffel bag and extracted the twenty-five-caliber pistol that Nelson had given me. The waistband of my trousers held the gun firmly at the small of my back. My jacket concealed it, and the weather was just right for jacket wearing.

There were no cars visible at Bonnie's house. The garage door was closed. I parked at the edge of her property, like I might be visiting the neighbor. Bonnie didn't know what kind of car I was driving, but Newark did, and I was counting on him not being there.

I walked back to the side door going into the garage. Through a small opening between the curtains, I could see there were no vehicles inside. I used the credit card again to open the door. They really ought to make side doors more difficult to break into. The door to the kitchen was unlocked, and I let myself into the main part of the house.

Even though I had searched the place on Friday afternoon and found nothing, an idea had been rolling around in my brain for a couple of hours and I needed to follow through on it. My idea involved a movie I saw where the killing gun had been hidden behind the toilet tank in the bathroom. Following the movie plot, I went straight to the master bathroom and found there was no space between the toilet tank and the wall. Oh well. I was glad I hadn't actually told someone about my idea.

I went into the guest bathroom and found a one-piece toilet whose tank was approximately three inches away from the wall. My hopes were buoyed. I put my face against the wall and just as though it had been scripted, there was a gun. It was standing vertically in a holder that had been glued to the back of the tank. She had seen the same movie.

I used my handkerchief to take the gun from its resting place. It was a nine-millimeter Glock. I released the clip and found a full magazine, which in this case was ten rounds. I inserted the clip and stuck the gun into my waistband on my right side. The chance of the cops finding a guy carrying a concealed weapon illegally is probably one in a hundred, but the chance of the cops finding a guy carrying two concealed weapons is probably several thousand to one. The odds were with me.

Not needing anything else from Bonnie's house, I let myself out the same way I went in and drove to Nelson's office.

I noticed the Venetian blinds were closed when I arrived at the office. I thought it unusual but then remembered Nelson had closed the office for a week. I parked on the street in front of the office and walked up to Nelson's suite, not really knowing what I expected to find. I just felt the need to check it out.

When the doorknob turned in my hand I recoiled as though I had touched a poisonous snake. I immediately reached for the twenty-five-caliber pistol at the small of my back and very cautiously entered the office. Ready for anything, I walked through the suite with my pistol at eye level, arms extended in front of, and to my left side.

The suite was empty. No bodies, alive or dead. The top of Nelson's desk was clear. So were the desk drawers and the contents of the main filing cabinet where Nelson kept his active files. The transmitter was still under his desk.

I went to Gina's desk. Her radio and telephone listening devices were gone from the top drawer. The remainder of the desk looked untouched. Just the usual junk a person collects, including remnants from lunches, cosmetic items and an old pair of sneakers.

I was sure the local PD had looked the place over and probably talked with Bonnie and Nelson.

I wondered why they hadn't contacted me. Gina was killed in the early morning hours of Friday and today was Sunday and not a word from the cops. Even though I took the Monterey trip, they could have found where I was staying and at least left me a note. I felt slighted.

That was relatively unimportant compared to what looked like Nelson running off like a thief in the night. And, on top of it, forgetting to lock the office door on the way out. I realized I didn't have Nelson's home phone number and I doubted if it would be listed. I took a look at Bonnie's address file and found his number and address under B for boss. Nelson's phone rang fifteen times without being intercepted by an answering machine. Not a good sign.

I left the office and drove to Nelson's house with the help of my Thomas Guide. As it turned out, his place was only a few blocks from Bonnie's house. I wondered if that was a coincidence.

Nelson lived in a rambling ranch-style house with red-barrel tile on the roof, and wide, wood Venetian blinds on all of the windows. His driveway curved around the house into the entrance of a three-car garage. There were no cars in front of the garage. Peeking into the garage through the small high windows on the doors revealed a well taken care of old-model Corvette in the second bay. I rang the bell at the back door without getting a response. I was not going to break into Nelson's place. One burglary was enough, and besides, I had no reason to snoop around Nelson's house. I turned from the back door to walk to my car and stopped in my tracks as a black Ford Crown Vic with an antenna on the trunk lid came around the garage.

The driver, a tall lanky guy about forty-five with a thick mustache, got out of the Crown Vic and approached me. While walking toward me he said, "How you doing today?"

It was a rhetorical question, and I treated it as such by not giving an answer. I didn't want to act nervous, belligerent, or overly cooperative. I wanted to appear to be an innocent, middle-of-the-road type of guy. Guilt does things to you. I was illegally carrying two concealed weapons, and that made me nervous. I felt like I thought a person would feel, being stopped by the cops, for running a red light while driving a car loaded with cocaine. I had already mentally reviewed the possibility of him wanting to search me for weapons or drugs. I was ready to challenge him by demanding he articulate whatever probable cause he had that would allow him to search me without violating my fourth amendment rights. A big yes for the constitution.

"Why don't you tell me your name?" he said in the way cops do to establish control.

"I'm Harry Caine, and I'm a private investigator. My client is the owner of this house. I dropped by to see if he was in."

I said this while getting my license out of my back pocket and opening my wallet, exposing my PI license in one window and my driver's license in the other.

"Mr. Caine." He said in a way that sounded like he had been looking for me. "I take it Mr. Nelson is not at home." He pulled his credentials from his coat pocket and showed me a badge and said, "I'm Detective Roberts, Mountain View PD. I left a message for you at your hotel. I'm glad I ran into you. I need to ask you a few questions regarding the shooting of Gina Wilson. I have information that you might have been the last person to see her alive."

His attitude was cordial and professional, and I could see he was not going to search me. "I mean aside from the shooter, of course."

"Of course." I said, sporting a very small smirk.

"What were the circumstances that put you with Ms. Wilson on the night she was shot?"

"It's a long story detective. I can give it to you now or come into your office whenever you want."

"Try right now. I'll stop you if gets too long."

As I did with Detective Clark, I laid out my story from the time I first met Zucker to the time I saw the money being printed. I added the part about Gina leaving a note for me at my hotel on the night she was shot. I also told him about meeting her that night, prior to the two of us going to her office, so she could let me look around for the report that I thought Kincaid had delivered to Nelson. I told Roberts of my meeting with Detective Clark and the fact that he had informed the Secret Service of the counterfeiting activity. The only things I didn't tell him about were my trip to Monterey and the possible involvement of Bonnie Bliss.

When I was through, I asked Roberts, "Could you tell me the caliber of weapon used to shoot Ms. Wilson?"

"Yeah, it was a twenty-five caliber pistol. Two shots to the head at close range. Anything else you want to add or ask?"

I made a negative motion with my head while tacitly trying to recover from finding that Gina was not shot with a 9mm weapon. Was I off base, or what? I needed to know the caliber of the weapon used to kill Martin. I was now chaffing at the bit to call Detective Clark. The twenty-five caliber pistol at the small of my back was burning a hole through my shirt.

I had given Roberts a lot to think about. He left after saying he would be in touch. I was reporting to so many law agencies that I felt like a parolee.

As soon as Roberts drove away I went to the nearest pay phone and called Detective Clark in San Mateo. When he answered, I said, "Detective Clark, this is Harry Caine. I......" Before I could continue, he said, "What's the matter, Caine, you couldn't wait until tomorrow?"

"I want to know one thing. What caliber weapon was used to shoot Theodore Martin?" I tried to make the question sound innocent. With a quick response Clark said,

"Well, that's simple enough, Caine. It was a twenty-five caliber pistol. One shot to the head at close range. Don't tell me, you found the gun."

"Thanks detective. I'll talk to you tomorrow about it." I hung up before he could say anything more. As I suspected, I could be carrying the murder weapon and my prints were all over it. I could hear Nelson denying that he gave me the gun.

I got back into my car and drove quickly to Bonnie's house. While thinking the 9mm pistol was the likely murder weapon, how could I have produced the 9mm gun and tied it to Bonnie without divulging the fact that I stole it from her house during the commission of a B&E? Now that I knew a twenty-five-caliber pistol was used to do both shootings, I had to return the 9mm gun quickly. I thought of throwing it away but things have a way of catching up to you when you least expect it. You never know who's watching or from where they may be looking. I wanted to put it back so there would be no possible connection between Bonnie's house and me. But I still had the problem of explaining how I got hold of the report Kincaid had prepared for Bonnie.

It had been about an hour since I left her house, and the configuration of the house was just as I left it. I parked my car in the same place as I had an hour ago, entered the house via the credit-card-in-the-garage-door trick and quickly went back to the guest bathroom. Just as I was taking the 9mm pistol out of my waistband, I heard the sound of a chair scrape against the floor. I guessed the noise came from the kitchen. My adrenaline was pumping and I immediately jumped into the bathtub, pistol in hand, and pulled the shower curtain closed as it had been before I got in. Odds were it was Bonnie, and I really didn't need to be caught prowling through her house. I heard a few more movement noises and then the nerve-jangling sound of the bathroom door squeaking as it swung toward the doorjamb. My heart was pounding. I knew the only way out was to give up. I sure as hell was not going to attack her for the sake of getting out of the house. I flung the shower curtain to the shower side of the tub and said,

"This isn't as bad as it looks Bon..." My statement was interrupted when I realized that the noise was caused by a very large, as in fat, cat trying to get behind the bathroom door to reach a piece of string. Again I was glad I hadn't told anyone of my plan. There could be a better way to make a living.

I stepped out of the tub and used my handkerchief to clean the gun, then replaced it behind the guest bathroom toilet tank. I felt relieved to get rid of it.

I stopped at Nelson's office on the way back to the hotel. His office door was now locked. What the hell was going on? Odds were Nelson had not been back to the office after cleaning out his stuff. The blinds were still drawn. It was a sure thing that Nelson, Bonnie and or Newark had been there. I didn't think the PD or the Sheriff's department would be coming around on a Sunday afternoon. I couldn't get in, and I'd had enough B&E. I was through for the day.

I needed some relaxation and Anne popped into my mind. I called her at her restaurant. She said it was her busiest time of the week. She had to be there until ten tonight and then needed to get some rest to be fresh for Monday. She wanted to see me, but tonight was not a good time for her. I told her I understood, making sure I masked the disappointment in my voice. Maybe our one-night stand meant a little more to me than it did to her. I pushed it out of my mind by telling myself I had more important things to think about, like a football game, or a TV movie.

21

The alarm went off at 8:00 a.m., and I got up like I was waiting for it. I left my room at 9:00 and was stopped by the desk clerk wanting to let me in on the hotel's payment policy. All bills must be paid on Monday morning. I had been at the hotel since early last Wednesday, which counted as a Tuesday night stay. I owed for six nights and for any other room charges that I might have incurred. Just my luck. Nelson had split. I sprung for the three hundred and forty-eight dollars out of my retainer money and didn't feel too bad about it considering I was in Silicon Valley. Not knowing when I would earn more money, I needed to keep my credit card debt to a minimum. I paid with cash and got a receipt in hopes of getting the money back from Nelson, which was not likely.

After eating breakfast, I had just enough time to get to San Mateo for my ten o'clock meeting with Detective Clark.

I was ushered into Clark's office the moment I arrived in the lobby. Looking more animated than usual Clark greeted me with, "I know you have some important stuff for me this morning, Caine. Right?"

"I do. Several things have happened since I last talked with you, and I need to bring you up to date."

I brought him up to date, including the opinions I had formed since showing up at Martin's house on Thursday morning shortly after Martin had been shot. I related the fact that I believed Bonnie was involved out of a compulsion to help her son in Daytona Beach, who was stuck in a nowhere job when he could be next in line for king of the garbage pile.

I told Clark of Bonnie's history with Zucker, Sr. and of Anthony Falcon's connection to the Zucker empire and to ENARC. I told him of Leon Sugg's plan to steal the fake money and the copy machines. Then came the *coup de grace*. As I looked at Clark I pulled Kincaid's report, the 8mm tape and Nelson's twenty-five caliber pistol from inside my jacket. I laid them side-by-side on his desk.

"I didn't mention the gun. I didn't think much about it until I found out that both killings were done with a twenty-five caliber weapon. Nelson gave it to me Saturday morning for protection saying that things could get rough. I haven't seen him since. It could be coincidence, but odds are that this is the gun that was used in both killings. Also, odds are that the only prints on the gun will be mine. I guess it's my word against Nelson's that he gave it to me. In Summary, I know that Nelson, Bonnie, and Kincaid are all involved, and it depends on what you can find out about the gun as to who gets implicated for the shootings. It appears that Kincaid stole Martin's copy machines and the paper that I innocently delivered to Martin. I have no indication that Newark has done any criminal act while he's been here, but I wouldn't bet on it. We need to find all four of them, and if I were you, I'd start first with the Secret Service and find what they got from Kincaid in San Diego, assuming they stopped the plane before it left the country. He might be able to lay the whole thing out for us."

Clark, looking interested but somewhat skeptical said, "You've jerked me around before, Caine. What makes you think I believe everything you just told me? I mean, the gun. How do I know you weren't sent here to whack Martin and then circumstances arose that caused you to whack Gina Wilson. I'm sure Nelson is going to deny he gave you the gun and on top of that, the gun will probably not even be registered to him or anyone remotely connected with him."

With that said, Clark picked up the phone and dialed an extension number. "Hi, Bill. Clark in homicide here. I need you to do a ballistics test on a twenty-five-caliber pistol and compare it with the slugs found in the Martin shooting. The weapon is in my office. Could you send someone up for it? Give Mountain View PD a call and ask them to send over the slug they found in the Gina Wilson shooting. See if it matches up to the same gun. Any problems let me know. And this is definitely a rush job, Bill. Yeah, I know, but what the hell can you do? Do it quick and I'll owe you."

About two minutes went by in silence. It was awkward but I didn't want to continue harping on my story. It tends to weaken one's position. I wanted him to have the next word. Before that word came there was a knock on his door.

A young blonde-haired female entered and asked if she could pick up the weapon that was to be tested in the Martin case. She carried an evidence envelope and was wearing latex gloves. She bagged the gun, made some notations on the front of the envelope and said it would take approximately one hour to make the Martin slug comparison. After the lab tech left the office, Clark said, "Anything else you want to get off your chest while we wait?"

To the less observant, his manner was that of a cop talking to a perpatrator from whom he was trying to get a confession. I now knew him well enough to detect that he was being sarcastic and was letting me know in his unsubtle way that I'd been talking too much. I'd been thinking about going back to Nelson's office to check it out and I said, "I think we ought to go to Nelson's office and look around. I think he's up to his neck in the counterfeiting scheme and possibly the murders too."

I felt strange talking about Nelson that way, but there was no other way to put it. It was the way things were stacking up. The fact that I could be so objective about Nelson's involvement told me how much of a friend I considered him to be.

Clark was looking at me like he was thinking that I was an outsider who had no business analyzing any evidence or theorizing about any aspect of this case. He said, "And what do you think we'll find at Nelson's office?"

"Let's go and see."

Clark looked steamed and what was bothering him was that he knew it was a good idea and it irritated him that he didn't suggest it first. He picked up the telephone, flipped open a black address book sitting beside the phone and dialed a number.

"Detective Roberts, please." Clark stared out of the window while waiting for Roberts to pick up. "Hey Roberts, how you doing on the Gina Wilson shooting?"

Several seconds elapsed before Clark said, "I have Harry Caine with me. He tells me you guys met yesterday at Nelson's house." Clark listened for a minute and then said, "Yeah, I know what you mean."

If I were paranoid, I would have interpreted Clark's comment as an agreement to something negative Roberts said about me. I let it go.

Clark continued, "Caine thinks Nelson has skipped. I want to check out his office and thought I better check with you first." After another few seconds and a few yeah's, Clark said, "Thanks, I'm bringing Caine with me. We'll be there in about twenty minutes." Clark hung up and said to me, "Don't look so smug, Caine. I would have done it on my own without your suggestion."

I thought to myself, '*I don't think so,*' but said, "I know. That's why you're a professional." There was no sarcasm in my voice, only in my heart. Clark accepted the comment as a compliment. I needed to watch my attitude.

Twenty-five minutes after Clark hung up with Roberts, we were parking our separate cars in the parking area in back of Nelson's office building. The building manager's office was on the first floor. He excitedly informed us that Detective Roberts of the Mountain View PD was already in Nelson's office. Was there something wrong? Had something happened to Mr. Nelson? Clark's answer to the building manager's questions was, "Just a routine police matter."

It was obvious by the casual manner in which Clark and Roberts greeted each other that they were old friends. Roberts greeted me by saying, "Hello, Caine, I guess you never did get to speak with your client. Know anything about where he may have gone?"

"Not a thing. I came by here twice yesterday. The first time the door was unlocked and second time it was locked. I noticed that Nelson's desk was cleared when I arrived the first time, which was about 2:45 p.m. I left the door unlocked when I left a few minutes later."

"Why did you come by here in the first place, seeing as how it was a Sunday and it was likely that no one would be here?"

"Just on the off chance that Nelson would be here. I had a few things to discuss with him. The reason I asked you yesterday about the caliber of weapon used in the Wilson shooting was because Nelson had given me a twenty-five caliber pistol on Saturday, and I had a nagging thought that it might be the murder weapon. Detective Clark is now running a ballistics test on it."

With a heavy sigh, Clark said, "Geez, Caine, what would I do without you? You can tag along but keep quite and don't touch anything if you don't mind. Okay?"

"Okay. But I was just answering the Detective's question."

I thought these two guys would be the ideal good-cop, bad-cop team, or maybe the smart-cop, stupid-cop team. I wasn't sure yet.

Roberts and Clark put on surgical gloves. Roberts began looking through drawers in Nelson's office. Clark was looking through documents in, and around, Gina's and Bonnie's desks. I was in Nelson's office standing around, because I wasn't sure if I should be helping. I noticed Nelson's desk phone had a LED display on the outside of the handset. Using my handkerchief, I picked it up and began scrolling through the most recent calls. Pushing the down arrow revealed the caller's name, the caller's telephone number and the date the call came in. The cops overlooked this one just as Roberts had just overlooked the transmitter under Nelson's desk. I was more than a little surprised when the third call displayed my sister Susan's information. The call was received Saturday morning at 9:45 a.m. I quickly jotted down her number in my notebook and put the notebook back in my jacket pocket. Why had Susan called Nelson on a Saturday morning at his office? I needed to call her, but before doing so I asked Roberts while pointing to Nelson's office phone,

"Okay for me to make a call from this phone?"

"Better use an outside phone, Caine. We don't want to contaminate any possible evidence here in case this place gets sealed up."

I agreed, saying I would be right back. I walked downstairs and called Susan from a payphone booth inside the bookstore at the corner.

I caught Susan at home, and she was surprised to hear from me.

"Two times in one week. How did I get so lucky?" She said.

"Because you have a terrific brother. It's always good to talk to you, but this call isn't purely social. I'm at Dan Nelson's office and his caller ID list shows that you called his office Saturday morning. I'm not sure, but it looks like Nelson has pulled up stakes here. I'm sure that he's nowhere to be found around here. I'd never ask you this unless it was important, Susan. Could you tell me why you called him?"

"You make it sound so mysterious, Harry. Yeah, I'll tell you. He called me Friday evening and left a message asking me to call. I returned his call on Saturday morning. I know what you're going to ask next. What did he want? Right?

"No one ever said you weren't smart."

"Like brother, like sister. He wanted to know if he could come over to see me and asked if it would be alright if he arranged to meet someone here. I told him he could, but that I was busy all weekend and the first time I had would be Monday when I'm off work."

"Did he say what time he planned on being there?"

"He said he'd be here at 1:00 p.m."

"I can't explain right now, Susan, but the person Nelson was going to meet at your house is not going to show up. I don't want you to leave the house with him after he arrives.

"Are you nuts? I wouldn't go to the grocery store with that guy."

"I'm glad to hear it. I'll probably be there before he arrives, but if I'm not, keep him there until I am. Don't tell him I'm coming. Okay?"

"Yeah, okay, but why?"

"He's involved in a messy business that he hoped to make a bundle on, and I think he got too greedy."

"That sounds like Dan. Is this little favor going to put me in any danger or in any trouble with the law? Be very objective about this, Harry."

"For sure it will not put you in any trouble with the law, and Nelson is not the violent type. I'm sure he has the utmost respect for you, just be alert."

"Get here as soon as you can, Harry. I don't want to be here with him for very long after what you've told me. And I'm sure what you've told me is the tip of the iceberg."

"Thanks, Susan. I knew I could count on you. I'm on my way in a few minutes."

It was now 11:30 a.m. and Susan's place was an hour away in a little town five miles south of Santa Cruz, called New Brighton Beach.

I went back to Nelson's office where Clark and Roberts were still poking around, but looking as though they were ready to leave. Just as I walked into the suite, Clark's phone rang.

"Clark here. Yeah, give it to me." Ten seconds went by before he said, "I'm not surprised. Thanks for the fast turn around." He hung up and stared at me and then looked at Roberts when he said, "Caine's twenty-five is the murder weapon. The Martin slug and the Wilson slug match the test shot perfectly. The only prints on the gun belong to Caine, and it's registered to Nelson. Caine's prints were in the state database because of his PI license and exposed weapons permit."

Turning his attention back to me, Clark said, "I know you said Nelson gave you the gun, Caine, and even though I think you're telling the truth we're going to need some proof. What do you think, Roberts?"

Without hesitation Roberts said, "It obvious to me that Nelson is running. We better find him or Caine here is going to have a hard time convincing a jury where he got the gun."

I couldn't imagine a better time to interject my little bomb. "I happen to know exactly where Nelson will be at 1:00 p.m. today." I said, trying not to be smug. "He used to have a thing for my sister, and he contacted her over the weekend setting up a visit for today at one o'clock. She doesn't know why he's coming to see her and neither do I."

"When and how did you discover that?" Roberts said.

"Simple, I saw her number on Nelson's caller ID just before I asked if I could make a call from here. I went downstairs and called her. I told her I'd be there by the time Nelson arrived."

"Where is there?" Clark said.

"New Brighton Beach, over by Santa Cruz, just off the beach road. She's a little alarmed. I gave her the idea that Nelson has put himself into some kind of trouble with the law. I think I should get over there, like right now, and I hope you'll both join me."

"You bet your ass we will. We're not about to let you go screw this thing up and let Nelson get lost." Clark said, and received an affirmative nod from Roberts. Both Detectives immediately called in their intentions to their respective offices.

The Building manager was waiting at the bottom of the stairs. Roberts ordered him to lock up Nelson's office and change the lock so nobody enters until he advises him otherwise. The building manager readily agreed and we were off.

I drove my rental. The detectives followed me in Roberts' vehicle. We went across the mountains ignoring posted speed limits, arriving at the turn off from the pacific Coast Highway onto the road going down to the beach at 12:35 p.m. Susan's street jutted off the beach road halfway between Highway 1 and the beach. The street was one block long and about a block off the beach. Just enough distance to be protected from an occasional winter storm. Sunsets were visible from her living room windows. It was the kind of place that makes a person want to get home after work, or not go to work at all. Her car was parked in the driveway; no other vehicles were present, including the local PD or Santa Cruz County Sheriff's Office. Neither

Roberts nor Clark had notified local law enforcement of our visit. They needed to watch their manners.

I got out of the car. Roberts and Clark motioned for me to wait as they exited their car, thinking I was going into Susan's house without them.

Roberts said, "Because of the ballistic test results, you claiming Nelson gave you the gun on Saturday, and the fact that it's registered to him makes him a prime suspect for both murders. We're going to take him in."

Clark joined in by saying, "That's right. So what we want you to do is tell your sister to act normal when he arrives and leave the front door unlocked. We're going to move the cars around the corner where we can still see the house. When Nelson goes in the three of us will follow."

I said okay to the plan and walked to Susan's front door as Roberts and Clark drove around the corner. Susan opened the front door before I reached it. She looked upset and said, "What the hell's going on, Harry? Who are those two guys you were talking with? Are we going to have a big scene here?"

Her rapid-fire questions flew over my head. I said, "I'll explain it all to you after Nelson gets here. Trust me. Everything will be all right. Just act normal when he arrives and I'll take care of the rest. You're not in any danger. The two guys with me are cops. Make sure to leave your front door unlocked after Nelson comes in. Okay?"

"I'm scared, Harry. What am I supposed to say to him?"

I put my arm around her shoulders and drew her close to me. "The three of us will be right outside, Susan. We won't let anything happen to you. Just engage him in small talk. You won't have to talk to him very long. Don't forget, leave the front door unlocked."

Susan muttered an okay, and then looked up at me and said, "You owe me, Brother."

I moved my car around the corner, parked behind the detectives' car, got out as their back door opened, tacitly inviting me into their car. From that vantage point we could see the driveway into Susan's house. I was excited. They were talking about the forty-niners.

22

It was fifteen minutes of boredom with Clark and Roberts. If they didn't know everything there was to know about professional football, you'd never know it by listening to them. At three minutes after one a black, four-door BMW rolled to a stop in front of Susan's house. Nelson got out and approached the front door. He had a spring in his walk and a smile on his face. He puts on a good front. Susan opened the door just as he started to knock. She looked and acted normal, except for stepping back and patting his shoulder when he moved in for a hug. She smilingly ushered him into the house. As soon as the front door closed, Clark and Roberts opened their doors and got out. I followed their leads and the three of us headed for Susan's front door.

Roberts reached the door first, opened it quietly and went into the house. Clark followed and I brought up the rear. To my surprise the living room was empty and voices were coming from the back of the house where a glassed in family room jutted off the living room at a forty-five degree angle. I motioned for the detectives to follow me.

Clark, if he could have said anything would have said no. But under the circumstances, he tightened his jaw and followed. We stopped short of going through the doorway into the family room.

Nelson was talking and we listened as he said, "It's really good to see you again, Susan. It's been a long time, eh?"

Susan muttered a soft response that was below our hearing threshold. Nelson continued, "I've been keeping Harry busy since he's been out here, but I guess he'll be going back to Daytona Beach today or tomorrow. I'll probably not see him again before he leaves, and I'd appreciate it if you would give him a message that I apologize for the way things worked out.

Susan's voice was higher pitched than normal as she said, "It sounds like either Harry screwed up or you screwed up. Which is it?"

"Just tell him what I said. He'll understand. But that's not why I'm here. I had a couple of reasons. First is that I wanted to see you again and secondly, I needed to have a place that I could feel was absolutely private. A man is supposed to meet me here to give me a suitcase that belongs to me. He should be here, about right now. I hope you don't mind me waiting for him."

"I have something to do in a half hour, but you're welcome to wait for him here until I have to go. What's the guys name you're waiting for?" Susan sounded calm and sincere. Her voice was back to its normal pitch.

"His name is Kincaid, and he'll probably be driving a van of some sort."

Suddenly, a new more meaningful picture of what was really going on flashed across my mind. I stored it as Roberts motioned for us to make our move.

We burst into the room. Clark and Roberts with their service revolvers in hand. If they knew Nelson as well as I did they'd know how silly they looked jumping into the room like an over-the-hill swat team.

The shocked look on Nelson's face was classic as he jumped up from the couch, mouth open, eyes wide. Susan's reaction was to back away from Nelson as far as she could get, which took her to the far corner of her family room. Roberts did the talking.

"Daniel Nelson, you're under arrest for suspicion of the murders of Gina Wilson and Theodore Martin. The weapon used in both murders is registered to you. Please put your hands behind your back."

Clark cuffed Nelson and Roberts read him his rights. Nelson was still in shock. It looked to me that neither Roberts nor Clark were going to ask Nelson any questions, and I had a few I wanted answered.

I said, "I don't know how you thought you could get away with this, Dan. I mean giving me the murder weapon was a little bit more than stupid. I don't get it, and why is Kincaid supposed to meet you here?"

Nelson collapsed onto the couch. I was relieved that he hadn't denied giving me the gun. He looked like a kid who had committed a crime and for the first time realized the seriousness of his act. His self-assured, arrogant bearing had deserted him. He was the picture of a broken man. You never know how thin the persona shell is until the chips are down. Knowing it's best to extract information from a perpetrator immediately following apprehension, before he can construct a cover lie, I said, "Why did you kill Martin and Gina?" My request earned a glare from Clark and Roberts.

With a shaky voice Nelson said, "I didn't kill Gina or Martin. I was only interested in the machines and the paper, and I don't even know where they are. I'm telling the truth. I'm sorry I got you into this thing, Harry, and I hope you'll forgive my abusing your hospitality, Susan."

Nelson was quiet and seemed to be recovering his normal confident personality. I could tell by the way he reacted to the arrest, and his willingness to talk, that he had very little experience handling criminal cases. Surprisingly, Clark and Roberts remained quiet, so I said, "How did you get hold of Martin's machines and the currency paper?"

"Kincaid came to me offering to sell me the machines and paper."

"Didn't you ask him how he came to have them in his possession?"

"He wouldn't tell me. He said he had the stuff, and if I wanted it, he could deliver it."

Roberts asked, "If you say you didn't kill Martin, didn't it occur to you that Kincaid may have killed him to get the machines and paper?"

"It may have crossed my mind."

"How much did you agree to pay Kincaid?" Roberts pushed on.

"One hundred thousand."

It was clear that Kincaid didn't really appreciate the value of what he was holding at the time he sold it to Nelson. He obviously acquired a better appreciation of the machines and authentic currency paper since then.

Clark then asked, "Did you pay him yet?"

Nelson gave Clark a look of submission, which I interpreted as Nelson's resignation from all that he held dear. He had given up. "No. I was to transfer the money to his account in a Miami bank when he delivered a suitcase to me here at Susan's house. He should be here any minute."

Clark again, "Don't hold your breath, Nelson, he ain't coming and the suitcase full of money is now in the hands of the Secret Service in San Diego. Did you really believe Kincaid would bring you the suitcase? Didn't it occur to you that this guy would cheat his own mother to make a financial gain?"

"I admit I was naïve about Kincaid. I didn't know anything about him, and I guess I was too anxious to get the stuff since I had a buyer waiting in the wings. I should have known better about Kincaid. I should have known better about this whole mess."

Nelson was beating himself up, probably in hopes that he would somehow be given a break.

Clark followed up with, "We think you had a hand in blackmailing Martin into using his machines to print the money. We know about your connection with Zucker and that Zucker sent the currency paper from Florida with Caine here."

"It's not like that at all. The first time I heard Martin was using his machines to print counterfeit bills was when Harry told me he saw the operation at Martin's office in Mountain View. I had no idea what was going on until Kincaid approached me with his offer to sell me the machines and the paper. I guess I got greedy and didn't think clearly. Anyway, I accepted the offer but I wasn't going to actually print counterfeit."

"What were you going to do then, resell it to a higher bidder?" Roberts said.

"I guess so." Nelson said, head hanging down.

"Well that's enough for me. I'm going to take him back to the station for questioning and then book him into county jail. Okay with you, Clark?" Clark responded immediately with, "You made the arrest. He's good for both murders so it's six of one and a half dozen of the other. Let's go."

With that said, Clark ushered a handcuffed Nelson out of the house while Roberts went for his car. Clark pushed Nelson's head down into the back seat just like on TV. I watched from inside the house.

Before leaving the house, I thanked Susan and let her know that I thought she had performed like a champ.

"Christ, Harry, did Dan really shoot two people and is he really involved in counterfeiting?" Susan said, her eyes wide and her face pale.

"It looks like he is involved with the counterfeiting or at least had intentions to counterfeit until Kincaid screwed him over. Kincaid left Monterey in a Lear jet Sunday morning on his way to Bogotá Colombia with the counterfeiting machines and the currency paper. I don't know the details, but I'm sure Nelson will tell all in a short while. As we witnessed, he's not the type to stand up under interrogation. I can't see him shooting anyone, and even though he gave me the gun that turned out to be the murder weapon, I can't believe that he would kill a person."

"Why and when did he give you the gun, before or after the murders."

"He gave me the gun on Saturday. Martin was killed early Thursday morning and Gina Wilson was shot and killed in her apartment parking lot about 2:00 a.m. Friday morning. Said he thought I needed some protection in case things got rough. I've got to get over to Roberts' office."

"Which one was Roberts?" Susan asked. I realized that in the excitement neither Roberts nor Clark were introduced to Susan in her own house. Cops and PI's have lousy manners. I said, "The thin one. The other one is Clark. Roberts is with the Mountain View PD and Clark is with the San Mateo County Sheriff's Office. I'll call you before I leave for Florida, and don't worry, you won't be bothered again unless they want you to testify about Nelson coming to your house and maybe how you knew him." I gave Susan a hug and a kiss and told her I loved her.

Susan's final comment before closing the door as I left her house was, "Next time you come visiting don't be working on one of your damn cases, Harry."

I drove like a bat out of hell and caught up with Roberts. I wanted to see what transpired with Nelson at the Mountain View PD. Roberts was apparently driving like a bat out of hell also, because I didn't catch him until we got to the northbound entrance of Highway 101 in San Jose, a couple of miles from his office.

23

I never had a close relationship with the local PD's in my previous life as a California PI. Probably because I'd never worked a combined counterfeit and double murder case before. Who has?

Knowledge is power, and I was sure that Clark and, to a lesser degree, Roberts, knew that I had more information than they did. Not being law enforcement, I knew I wouldn't be included in questioning Nelson, but I wanted to make sure my questions were asked and answered as a matter of closure to Nelson's part in the crime.

I parked in a visitors space at the back of the Mountain View PD, and caught up with Roberts and Clark as they took Nelson out of their car. We all walked in together with Nelson leading the way, being guided by Roberts' hand on his shoulder. Nelson looked around at me on the way into the station with a pleading look in his eyes, as if to say, 'Do something, I didn't kill any one.' The scene had a surreal quality about it that I didn't like so I brought the picture back to earth by thinking, *'Hey, you're the one who did the shooting, don't look at me for help.'* But of course it wasn't clear that he did the shooting. Basic character doesn't change abruptly, and I didn't believe Nelson's character included killing.

Just as we got inside the station, Clark's cell phone rang. He answered, "Oh yeah, Lewis, go ahead."

At the mention of Lewis' name, I stopped with Clark while Roberts continued on with Nelson. There were a lot of uh-huhs and ummm's before Clark said, "Okay. Thanks for the info. It helps. By the way, what's happening to the east coast branch of this operation?"

Clark looked at me with raised eyebrows while listening to what Lewis was telling him. In a voice that said okay, that's the end of the conversation, Clark said, "I'll tell Caine. I'm sure he's dyin' to know. Thanks again." Clark hung up and stared at me.

"What?" I said, prompting him. "What did he say"?

"Well, they picked Kincaid up at the airport in San Diego. They took every thing off the plane and impounded it at a federal hanger in San Diego. Kincaid is in a federal detention center near there. They charged him with intent to defraud the federal government and possession of counterfeit currency with intent to distribute. There was also a Colombian guy on the plane that they put away. The pilot claimed he was just the chauffeur and knew nothing about what he was carrying or why he was carrying it. Could be true. They let him go but will follow up on him. The important thing for us is that they got Kincaid. The feds probably consider catching the Colombian was the big deal. Kincaid laid out quite a story."

"For Christ's sake, detective, I developed the information they acted on. I have a right to know what's going on." Sometimes, being indignant works. However, I knew that in a cop's mind I didn't have a right to anything when it comes to what they want, or don't want, to give out.

Clark held me in his gaze for a few seconds. As though he just made a decision, he said, "I'd better go tell Roberts what Lewis got from Kincaid before he beats Nelson into the ground. You'll know in due time, Caine. Relax. You can come down to the interrogation room, but you can't go inside or listen while we're questioning Nelson." Clark was enjoying holding out on what Kincaid had said.

We walked through the 'DO NOT ENTER' door and down the hall to room 'A'. The upper portion of the door to room 'A' was glass. Nelson was sitting facing the door on the far side of a six-foot worktable. Roberts was sitting on the other side with his back to the door. It looked like a small conference room instead of a room dedicated to questioning suspects. I didn't see the standard one-way mirrored wall. Maybe they didn't get many suspects to interrogate at this station. I wanted to know what Kincaid told Lewis, and I didn't intend to let Clark out of my sight until I found out.

Clark tapped on the glass to get Roberts' attention. Roberts came out while Nelson sat with a hangdog look. I looked away from Nelson and concentrated on what Clark was about to tell Roberts.

"Okay, Caine. I guess you can hear this if it's okay with Roberts." Clark gave Roberts a look that tacitly asked if he thought it was okay for me to hear. Roberts gave a slight nod with a tight-lipped look that said 'of course'. The look could have also meant 'of course, stupid".

Clark began, "According to Agent Lewis of the royal Secret Service..."

Clark paused for effect to let us know that he knew we all felt the same way about the feds, be they Secret Service, FBI, Sky Marshals or whatever. As you get to know people, their prejudices and insecurities bubble to the surface, like a bathroom cleanser, scrubbing away the façade.

Satisfied that he had made his point, Clark continued, "Kincaid sang like a bird when the feds told him he was in the hot seat for the Wilson and Martin murders, in addition to the counterfeit rap."

Roberts chimed in, "God, I remember Kincaid when he was a reputable PI. He caught his wife having an affair with an investigator who was working for him. She ran off to Vegas with the guy, divorced Kincaid and married the investigator. Kincaid never got over it. Used to dress sharp and run a tight agency. Now he looks like a slob and only gets work other PI's won't take. I doubt that he still has his PI license. Everybody has a story."

Clark continued, "As I was saying, he sang like a bird and the song was a confirmation of everything Caine has told me."

For Roberts' benefit Clark continued the story Lewis had told him, and in fact it was a confirmation of everything I had thus far told Clark.

"Kincaid was hired by Bonnie Bliss to do surveillance on Martin. The information he developed in the form of a video tape was used to blackmail Martin into printing phony money with his machines. I have the tape and it's a lulu. My guess is that rather than take the chance on having his career ruined at SRI, Martin agreed to print the counterfeit money."

Roberts asked, "What's on the tape, Caine?"

"It's Martin giving oral sex to a guy in a porn shop movie booth. I guess Martin never came to grips with his sexual orientation and assumed no one else would be able to, either."

Clark continued, "Kincaid's story tracks with what Caine has told me, and, thanks to Caine, I have the report Kincaid delivered to Bonnie Bliss that set this whole thing in motion. The report clearly shows that Bonnie Bliss hired Kincaid, and that Kincaid delivered his sex tape to Bonnie."

Clark forgot to include the fact that I told him that I thought Bonnie had planted the tape in Nelson's desk so he could take the rap for killing Martin when the tape was found. I'm sure he didn't want me getting credit for everything. Who likes to look stupid?

Clark continued, "Here's the deal with Nelson. He didn't have anything to do with the killings because he didn't have a motive. According to Kincaid, he wasn't involved in the blackmail and didn't know about the counterfeiting until Caine told him about it."

In an attempt to show ownership, or at least that I was involved in developing the information Clark was throwing out, I said, "Thank you".

Clark continued, "According to Kincaid, Nelson was innocent as a newborn. Bonnie had Kincaid steal the machines and paper from Martin's store front on El Camino. He was supposed to deliver them to Bonnie's house, but he got greedy and went into business for himself. Instead of taking the machines to her house, Kincaid offered the machines and paper to Nelson for one hundred thousand dollars. Also, according to Kincaid, Nelson stalled for a day and then agreed to buy the stuff from Kincaid at that price, provided Kincaid delivered the stuff to the Monterey Airport. The guy he was delivering to was the pilot of the Lear jet. He was going to fly the machines and paper down to Colombia. When Kincaid delivered the machines and paper he was supposed to pick up a brief case and deliver it back to Nelson at an address in Brighton Beach. But being the smart greedy bastard that Kincaid is, he knew immediately that Nelson had sold the stuff and that the brief case would contain the money Nelson was being paid for the machines and paper. It just so happens that the guy Nelson sold the machines to is one Tomas Escobar Fuentes, the dealmaker for the largest counterfeiting operation in the world. They run their operation out of Bogotá Colombia and are responsible for about half of the phony one hundred dollar bills that are circulating in this country right now."

It's disconcerting when you hear your own words coming back at you without being given credit. Apparently never to stop, Clark continued, "How Nelson made contact with Fuentes is yet to be determined. Fuentes was on the plane to deliver the money in Monterey after checking out the quality of the printed bills. Kincaid told Fuentes that Nelson had directed him to go to San Diego with the plane, and that Nelson was going to pick up the money from Kincaid at a place near San Diego. Kincaid's pretext was good enough that Fuentes bought it. And, if it weren't for Caine, Kincaid would have pulled it off."

Now that was more like it, so I gave Clark another, "Thank you."

Clark let us know that the brief case Kincaid picked up contained two million real bucks. It was clear to me that Nelson was planning to change venues after getting hold of the two million. It was also clear that Kincaid wanted a ride to San Diego where he would start his disappearing act along with the two million. When Clark was finished, he added the esoteric remark, "What'a you think about them apples?"

He waited for a comment from either of us. I spoke first. "It's clear that Nelson didn't have a motive to kill Martin or Gina and neither did Kincaid. Kincaid just reacted to his greed instinct and took the machines for himself, two times. He stiffed Bonnie, and then he stiffed Nelson. Bonnie set up the whole counterfeiting operation. She probably killed Martin because he got cold feet and wanted out. She had to pop Gina because she found out that Gina was blabbing about the counterfeit operation to her boyfriend. She was probably afraid that Suggs intended to take over the counterfeiting operation for his militia group. And, by the way, she was right.

Roberts spoke up, "Now that everyone's on the same page, I think we ought to find out where Nelson kept his twenty-five-caliber pistol. The most likely scenario, is that Bonnie stole the gun from Nelson's office after being contacted by Martin. Martin probably told her he was not going to print any more money after he finished the first batch on Wednesday night and early Thursday morning. Pangs of conscience, or something like that. She had to take quick action to see to it that he continued. He probably held fast and threatened to expose her as a blackmailer, and she killed him. After all, based on what Caine has told us, she had to make sure that Moshe, JR. was reinstated to his rightful place in the family's crime business. She probably believed that Junior had to make his old man proud before the old man would reinstate him. According to Caine, she considered his exile to the boat yard a disgrace."

Clark now accepted all I had to say after hearing the confirmation of my earlier suppositions from Lewis. I started to fill Roberts in on Moshe Zucker's father and the father's nefarious business connections that reached all the way to ENARC. Roberts stopped me by saying, "Don't bother, Caine, Clark laid that all out for me the other day." Hooray for interagency cooperation.

Roberts said, "Why don't we go ask Nelson about where he kept the twenty-five caliber pistol and how he got connected with Fuentes. I want you in on this, Caine, so I don't have to explain to you later what was asked and answered. But you are not to ask any questions. Got it?"

I nodded in the affirmative and the three of us walked into the room. Nelson perked up. Roberts took the lead by saying, "Okay, Nelson, looks like you might get a walk on the murders. Thanks to Kincaid's confession, it appears that you had nothing to do with the murders of Martin and Wilson."

It wasn't very prestigious having Kincaid the slob confirming my theories on the crimes.

Instead of a relief sigh or a thank you, Nelson said, referring to Kincaid, "You can't trust anyone these days."

Roberts continued, "Yeah, the Secret Service caught him, along with Tomas Escobar Fuentes, Martin's copy machines, the paper, and three-hundred thousand dollars in counterfeit twenties. Lewis said the twenties were good enough to be successfully passed anywhere. Only slight variations allowed the feds to determine that the twenties were counterfeit."

I immediately calculated that at least sixty-thousand dollars of counterfeit twenties were missing, if what Lewis said was true. Very interesting. I knew it couldn't be Kincaid or Fuentes who took the counterfeit. There would have been no time for them to hide the money, and there would be a body search going into the federal detention center. It probably wasn't the pilot since he wouldn't have had access to the money. Too busy piloting the plane. It could have been one of the feds making a little score. Who said government employees are not colorful?

Roberts, with perceptively less interest continued, "You are not a suspect in the two murders, Mr. Nelson, but we and the Secret Service have substantial evidence that you are guilty of intent to defraud the federal government, so we're going to have to turn you over to the feds and they'll take you to a federal detention center.."

Roberts asked Nelson, "You gave Caine a twenty-five caliber pistol that turned out to be the weapon that killed both Martin and Wilson. Now I know you didn't do the shootings and I want to know where you had that pistol before you gave it to Caine."

Nelson was being very cooperative in attitude and body language. He sat upright and looked Roberts in the eyes and said, "I could refuse to say anything further and demand an attorney, but I'll cooperate, as I've been doing all along, for any future consideration you can give me." Looking back at me, Nelson continued, "I had the gun in a holster, taped up under the swivel chair in my office. I took it from there just prior to Caine coming to my office on Saturday morning."

"Did anyone other than you know the gun was there?" Roberts said.

"Yes, it was Bonnie's idea to put it there. We were occasionally worried that an irate litigant would burst into the office with the intent to revenge an action that went south. We thought it best to have some protection on hand for that possibility."

Under his breath I heard Clark mutter, "Only a lawyer could have said it like that."

"How did you make contact with Tomas Escobar Fuentes in order to sell him the machines and paper?" Roberts asked.

Nelson responded immediately. "These guys don't miss a beat. When Fuentes contacted me by telephone, he said that he saw the patent pending application on a federal trademark and patent database. He saw my name and address associated with the patent pending and contacted me."

"How did he find out what the capabilities of the machines were?" Roberts asked.

"When he called, I discussed the machines with him since the information was already public. He was a pleasant sounding guy. He said he wanted to be able to sell the machines in his South American country. I didn't ask him where he was from. When I was talking to him, I had in mind that ultimately I would be helping Martin sell his machine. I recall telling him what the advantage the machines had over traditional copiers. He was very interested and said that if I ever wanted to negotiate a sale of those machines to let him know. He left me a private number and told me to call anytime. So when Kincaid offered to sell me the machines after Martin's death, I started making bad decisions and here I am."

"Do you have any questions, Mr. Nelson?" Roberts said. Nelson's simple and dejected response was, "No."

Nelson looked at me and said, "What can I tell you, Harry, I went for it and didn't make it."

Feeling that the interrogation was over, I said, "It's bad enough not making it when you're going for the right thing, but going for the wrong thing and not making it is the worst. What did you expect to do with the two million? I mean, were you going to leave the area? Is that why you cleaned out your files and your desk? And what about your house and your career? What the hell were you thinking about, Dan?"

"I admit the money turned my head. It's a weakness. I was going to make arrangements to close down my practice but I wasn't going to leave the area. I was going to play it by ear and see what developed as a result of having a couple of million bucks stashed away. I took my current files so I could complete each one or get it reassigned to another attorney. It's not that I don't have a conscience, Harry, I just have a weakness for the easy buck. I'll have time to work on that character flaw now."

He was being objective about his own character. A point for him. I was being objective about my character also when my thoughts went to recouping the expense for the hotel room. I said, "So we don't part company with any loose ends, you owe me for the hotel expense which I had to pay this morning. Three-hundred and fifty bucks."

Okay, so I made a two-dollar profit. I considered it round off. At the mention of the hotel expense, Nelson pulled a checkbook from his coat pocket and wrote me a check for the three fifty. I would take it to the bank immediately. You don't know who to trust these days. I nodded an implied thank you, and said, "If you ever need a PI again, don't call me. Good luck Dan."

I walked out of the room followed by Clark, who led me to the side of the hallway and said, "Just a minute, Caine. I want to say a few things." I was braced for a blast. Probably for butting into police business, or just generally being a smart ass in the eyes of the local fuzz, . It goes with the business. Clark continued, "It's rare that a civilian gets so involved with any of our investigations and I'm always skeptical about it. I'm sure it showed. Anyway, I want you to know you did a good job. We appreciate it. I'll find Bonnie Bliss and bring her in. She had the motive, opportunity and weapon for both killings. We need to clear up a few things with her son, and I guess I'll have to go to D.C. to do it. By the way, I didn't mention it to either you or Roberts, but Lewis told me they picked up Zucker, Jr. at the Daytona Boat Yard, Anthony Falcon at his place in Fernandina Beach, and Michael Lawrence at the ENARC plant in Massachusetts. The three of them are being held at a federal detention center in D.C. Lewis told me that he believes you didn't know what was in the packages you delivered from Daytona, and as a result, no charges. It's the least they could do after what you've done for them. As far as I'm concerned, Caine, you can go back to your boat any time you want. I want you to let me know where I can contact you if we need to pull you out here for court testimony."

Clark was being paged by the operator. He answered the call. From what he said, I could tell there were media people waiting for him in the lobby. He wished me good luck, and walked away.

'Go back to your boat anytime you want' were the words I was waiting to hear. The hell with Bonnie, and who cares about Newark; wherever they are. Clark and Roberts will find them. As far as I was concerned, I played a significant role in solving a double-murder and providing evidence that resulted in the break-up of a counterfeiting operation, not to mention setting up the Secret Service to nab a key figure in the Colombia counterfeiting world. It was a little bothersome that I couldn't actually hand Bonnie over to the cops and tie up that big loose end.

Heading out of the Mountain View PD station, I realized I had already missed check out time and decided to make a flight reservation back to Daytona Beach for sometime tomorrow. I needed to turn in the car at the San Francisco airport before departure. I should have charged Nelson for the car rental. I was slipping. I didn't believe I would be given permission to talk to Nelson again today, so I rationalized that I had made enough from him. Forget it. Go home.

I was crossing the parking lot to get to my car when I heard someone yelling my name. I turned and saw a female with a microphone in her hand, followed by a cameraman jogging across the lot. "Mr. Caine, Mr. Caine."

I stopped. The reporter, a bright looking blonde in her late twenties, caught up and said, "Detective Clark told me you were responsible for breaking up a counterfeit ring and for finding evidence that points to the shooter in the recent deaths of Theodore Martin and Gina Wilson. Is that true?"

I gave her an affirmative nod and waited for her next line, which was, "I'd like to get a photo of you for tomorrow's paper. I'll get your information from Detective Clark. Okay?"

"Sure. Fire away."

I guessed Clark told her to come back to him to get the story, so I wouldn't take too much credit or say something out of line. Cops are control freaks.

I didn't think I'd be coming back to California to work as a PI, so I posed for the photo. After three shots, the reporter thanked me and sprinted back into the building to get the rest of her story.

I got into the car and headed back to the hotel, making a stop at Nelson's bank. I thought of calling Anne. What better way to spend my last night in California? The thought was pushed aside by the little guy in the back of my head that said don't make more of it than it was. I never go wrong when I listen to the little guy, so I listened.

I'd had enough of the San Francisco Bay Area hustle and bustle. My trip let me see California in a different light and made the Florida east coast look inviting, the humidity notwithstanding. A testimony to the concept, you can't go home again.

DAVID SHAFFER

I would say to anyone waiting for me to visit the Bay Area again, don't count on it.

24

Knowing I was going to check out in the morning made going back to the hotel feel good. Chances are I wouldn't have a problem getting a flight out of San Francisco on Delta. I might have to take a roundabout way to Daytona Beach, but come hell or high water, I was leaving tomorrow.

I retrieved the open ended return ticket from my duffel bag and called Delta Reservations. The travel gods were being good. There was an open seat on tomorrow's 3:00 p.m. flight from San Francisco to Dallas and an available seat on the connecting flight out of Dallas to Daytona Beach. As they say, I'm out'a here. A steak dinner this evening followed by a movie. Turn in early and up in the morning at nine. Check out at eleven. Turn the car in at twelve and hang out at the airport sipping a mind numbing martini or two before taking off. That was the plan.

It was 4:15 p.m. Too early to eat and go to a movie, but not too early for a mid-afternoon nap. It was one of those times when everything was in order. No pressure and no money worries. Life was good.

There were no messages for me at the lobby desk, and I informed the desk clerk that I was checking out in the morning. I could have waited until morning to tell him but I felt like I had stayed too long and was glad to let him know that I did have somewhere else to live. I got into my room, striped down to my shorts and stretched out on the bed. I hadn't quite uncurled my toes when there was a knock on the door. I wasn't expecting anyone and there was no peephole in the door. I put on my pants and opened the door. There stood Leon Suggs.

It had been three days since I last saw Suggs and he looked every bit as angry now as he had then. I was right about the anger. As soon as we recognized each other he crashed through the door, greasy boots, greasy jeans, chains and keys rattling with each step, slamming the door behind him. From nowhere he had a big ass .45 with a silencer pointed at my midsection. I looked at him, waiting for his first line, which was. "You may not like this, scum bag, but you're going with me." By way of continuing our Friday fight, he followed with, "You're not so tough now, are you dick-head?"

Since I was going with him for whatever reason, I was sure he wasn't going to shoot me. Secure in that knowledge, I couldn't resist saying, "It's not that I'm any less tough, I merely want to hold off breaking your neck until you put the gun away."

Suggs' face flushed. To sting him a little deeper, knowing he couldn't have the answer to what I was about to ask him, I said, "Did you ever find out who whacked your old lady?"

That caused his gun hand to tremble like he was holding himself back from pulling the trigger. I'd probably pushed him far enough. Without gaining composure, Suggs said, "You fuckin' know I did. We'll talk about that later. Get dressed, now, before I blow your head off."

I got dressed, put my keys in my pocket, and walked out the door in front of him. He slammed the door closed and we headed to his truck. He walked between the lobby desk and me with his gun pressed into my side. His effort to hide the fact that he had me at gunpoint was wasted. The lobby was empty.

I couldn't miss Suggs' truck. It was the one with the driver's door kicked in. I got in the driver's side. Suggs pushed me to the passenger side as he entered the truck. He put his gun in his left hand and dropped that hand into his lap with the gun pointing at my gut.

He drove to the 280 and went north. When he took the turnoff to Half Moon Bay I knew we were headed for his place in Pillar Point. Thirty minutes later, and without any talking on the way, we drove up the ramp onto the wharf running beside Suggs ex-cannery residence.

I was beginning to get concerned about his motive for forcing me to go with him. Now that we were here, all bets were off as to when he would shoot me. He got out of the truck and, without taking his eyes off of me, walked around the front, opened the passenger side door and jerked me out of the truck. I was prodded with the barrel of the .45 to go into the doorway at the wharf level and walk up the stairs into his living quarters.

Suggs had been busy. With eyes as big as half dollars, and duct tape over their mouths, Bonnie and Newark sat looking at me with their backs against a four by four support toward the front of the room. Their hands were tied to the four by four and their feet tied to rings that were through bolted on the floor in front of each of them. Newark's right leg was covered with blood from the thigh down. A blood-red rag was tied around his thigh, and he looked pained. It was like seeing a couple of old friends, except that old friend Bonnie was now wanted for questioning in Gina's and Martin's murder. I didn't want to give Suggs any provocation to shoot them if he didn't already know that Bonnie shot Gina.

To stall for time, I said, "I don't know about those two but I've got other things to do, Suggs. What's the point? What the hell do you want?"

Suggs' nostrils flared and his face blanched. It was the body language that meant, I'm going to shoot you, now. I needed to diffuse him before he exploded.

"If it's the machines and paper you want, I know where they are."

It wasn't a lie. I just left out a few things.

"That's what I want, stupid. That, and the head of Miss dumb-ass killer here."

If he hadn't said it with so much vengeance and latent violence the statement would have sounded childish. There was no doubt that he was saying that Bonnie killed Gina, and there was also no doubt that she was in for it. She was probably the main course at this little dinner party.

"What makes you think Bonnie had anything to do with Gina's death?" I needed to verify that he meant what I thought he meant, and I needed to stall until I could figure out a way to disarm him.

"I guess it won't make any difference now because all you motherfuckers are going to die. We're getting the machines and there's going to be a payback for Gina. You and the wise guy here just happened to be in the wrong place at the wrong time. I'll tell ya how I know. Listen up, maybe you'll learn a few tricks from me, eh?"

"That's possible." I said while thinking it wasn't very likely. I could have also corrected his logic about being in the wrong place at the wrong time. Actually we were in the wrong place at the right time, relative to Suggs. A small point that I didn't think necessary to bring up right now.

With bravado, Suggs continued, "I've been following her around. I knew she would lead me to the machines. I went over to Nelson's office Sunday and let myself in to see what was in there. You know what I'm sayin'? I didn't see nothin' interesting, and, when I was gettin' ready to drive away, I saw Bonnie here walking into the building with Newark. It looks like super-bitch and Newark work for the same guy. I heard her tellin' Newark about everything she done. That includes her shooting Martin and Gina and trying to frame Nelson for it. She also had your detective pal, Kincaid, steal Martin's stuff. What she said was being transmitted right out from under Nelson's desk to my ear through my truck radio. Seems like the cops didn't search Nelson's office very good.

Suggs paused as though he thought he had just delivered the ultimate zinger. He got no reaction, and continued with, "And, what's more stupid, is that Bonnie bitch knew the damn thing was under there because she had listened to you and Gina in Nelson's office the night Gina was shot. I heard her tell Newark she found the transmitter when she planted Kincaid's tape of Martin in Nelson's desk. Hearing what you and Gina talked about was the reason she shot Gina. She told me the whole story after I laid a round in Newark's leg, so I could haul his ass over here in my truck. I guess she was afraid I'd do the same to her if she gave me a hard time.

Suggs reflected for a moment, and said, "The transmitter was my idea. I showed Gina how to hook it up and how to listen to it. Guess her getting shot could be partly my fault. Still, there was no call for Bonnie to shoot Gina just because she knew a little about the counterfeiting."

I thought Suggs to be the master of the understatement when he said that Gina getting shot could have been partly his fault. Suggs cut his eyes over to Bonnie, and shouted, "Bitch!" He walked over to the tied up pair and ripped the duct tape from their mouths, leaving big painful looking red rectangles. Looking at Bonnie, he continued, "She played all you educated guys, but she didn't play me. You know why? Because I'm too fuckin' smart. There's lots of ways to be smart, ya know. I got an education on the street. You might even say I have a street PhD, because I'm one street-smart son-of-a-bitch."

I didn't know how smart he was, but I did know he was a son-of-a-bitch. I get off-the-wall thoughts in times of severe stress and I was now thinking that Suggs' street PhD could be referred to as an StD. Odds are he had one of those.

"Bonnie told me you would know where the machines are. Isn't that right, Bonnie?"

Newark remained silent and Bonnie answered with, "Yes, you demented bastard. Gina was lucky to leave this world just to get away from you. I did her a favor, and if I could get free from here, I'd do you a favor, too."

Suggs backhanded her across the face, making her nose bleed. She didn't flinch. This was one tough woman. Her reaction to the backhand was to spit at Suggs, but her trajectory was off making the effort a symbolic gesture that got a reaction. Suggs swiftly put the gun to her head, his hand shaking, and beads of sweat visible under his nose.

"This ain't the law office, bitch, you're not in charge here. I want you to tell Caine why you shot Martin and Gina, just like you told Newark in Nelson's office yesterday."

All of a sudden, I was beginning to think there was a method to Suggs' madness. He was going to make sure she fried for the two killings no matter what happened to him. He probably figured he would have to go into hiding once he got hold of the machines and he looked at me as a person on the side of the law who would do the right thing.

Suggs shouted at Bonnie, "Tell him bitch! You're so proud of it!"

Bonnie glared at him and then looked me in the eyes and said, "I know I'm going to die, so I'm going to tell you what I've done. I hope you will let my son know what I did for him. It'll show him how much I love him."

Bonnie paused for a little dramatic effect, then looked at me and said, "I did what I had to do to make sure Mo would succeed in this operation he dreamed up out of his fertile imagination. I was blackmailing Martin with the videotape I got from Kincaid. He had agreed to print all five cartons of currency paper to keep me from turning the tape over to senior management at SRI. After printing the first batch, he decided he was not going to use his machines to print any more counterfeit money. He couldn't stand the guilt. He wouldn't listen to reason, and he wouldn't accept my offers to help him. He was going to turn Mo and me into the feds. I had to get rid of him. I'm sure you understand. Once I'd done that, I wasn't going to let that loud mouth Gina stand in my way of seeing Mo restored to his rightful place in his father's business."

With that said, Bonnie paused again, making her jaw tight as though to say, 'that's the kind of character I have.' Her attempt at martrydom didn't impress anyone, and staring at the ground, she continued. "I heard everything you and Gina talked about in Dan's office the night she let you go through the files and through Dan's desk. I was parked across the street listening on my car radio to the transmitter in Dan's desk. When Gina drove away, I followed her to her apartment house and made sure she wouldn't interfere again. Mo's plans are not something that ordinary people can mess with. Don't you understand, he's a genius and he has to succeed?"

I knew, if I survived this thing, that I would likely be required to testify in court to what she was saying. While she was in a talkative mood, I asked, "When did you take the twenty-five caliber pistol from under Nelson's chair?"

"I went to the office early Thursday morning and took the gun. I was on my way to see Martin. He had called me at six o'clock in the morning to tell me he was through using his invention for counterfeiting, and I asked him if I could come over and talk to him about it. He said it would be no use, his mind was made up, but I convinced him to talk to me in person. I got there about seven o'clock. We talked but he wouldn't change. I had no choice but to kill him. He said he was going to contact the feds, tell them everything about the blackmail and the counterfeiting. He was going to cause Mo to look like a fool in the eyes of his father. I just couldn't let that happen. After I shot him, I went back to the office and planted Kincaid's tape behind one of Dan's desk drawers. I knew it would be found and cause the police to believe Dan had killed Martin. It was then that I found the transmitter in Dan's desk. It dawned on me then why Gina was always listening to her radio with the earphones. I tested it out by turning on her radio without changing the frequency setting and buzzed Dan's interoffice telephone. I decided to leave the transmitter where it was and I was glad I did. I didn't leave the gun because I was worried that someone would come in early and find what I was doing. I called Kincaid and instructed him to pick up the machines and paper and deliver them to my house. He had already found out where Martin was doing the printing. I made the mistake of trusting Kincaid. It was late that night when I came back to the office to put Dan's gun back under his chair. I could tell that someone was in the office even though the blinds were drawn. Light was visible around the edges of the blinds, and I knew that no lights were on when I left at the end of the workday. I tuned my car radio to the transmitter's frequency and heard you and Gina talking about the machines being used to produce the counterfeit bills. I waited until Gina came out. When you drove off, I followed her to her apartment and shot her. No loud mouth little tramp is going to destroy my son's chances for a better life."

    She had said these things with obvious pride in the belief that she had done what was best for her son.

    I looked at Suggs. His eyes were burning a hole in Bonnie. A beat after she finished, Suggs, almost spitting the words from his clentched teeth, said, "You're lucky I don't blow your fuckin head off." It was said with a ferocity that discouraged any further comment.

25

In an attempt to lighten things up a bit, I said, "How are you doin' Newark?" Newark's face was in a deep frown. He acted as though he were in a stupor. I guessed partly because of the pain in his leg and partly because he was worried about how to explain this turn of events to his boss. He had been silent since Suggs ripped the tape from his mouth. He need not have worried so much, because his boss undoubtedly already knew about the Secret Service picking up his son, Anthony Falcon, and Michael Lawrence at ENARC. Zucker Sr. probably felt relieved that he wasn't in the round up. After this fiasco, boat-yard Zucker would almost certainly be relegated to the boat yard controller's job for the rest of his civilian life, much to the chagrin of Momma Bonnie. Newark might get chastised for not keeping me under control, but then, too much was expected of him.

Suggs was still holding the gun, not pointing it at anyone, just holding it. He had the orbs to shoot Newark in the leg, but my money said he couldn't have killed him. His tough-guy persona was an act. Whether or not Suggs was aware of it, he had insured Bonnie was on her way to the lock up, probably for the rest of her life, when he made her tell me all that she had done in the name of helping her son. I figured that was exactly what he wanted to do, at some level of consciousness.

To test my theory, I said to Suggs, "Can I talk to you in private?"

"Why the fuck do you think I'd want to talk to you in private? I ain't got time for talking privately. Tell me where the damn machines are before I blow your head off."

"That's what I want to talk to you about. Could we step outside for a minute? I think you'll want to hear what I have to say."

With a sigh of disgust, and without looking me in the eyes, Suggs nodded toward the door. We walked out onto the landing and he said, "I'm getting real irritated, Caine. And when I get irritated someone usually gets hurt. If what you have to tell is not about where the machines are, you're finished. You hear?"

"Yeah. I hear. Now put that damn gun away and listen to me."

Suggs let his gun hand drop to his side. So far, so good. I continued, "This is going to come as a big disappointment, Suggs, but the machines, paper and even the phony currency that Martin printed Wednesday night were confiscated by the Secret Service in San Diego earlier today. The feds got Kincaid, some Colombian guy he was selling the machines and paper to, and the Lear Jet they were using to get to Colombia."

I let that sink in. Suggs was quiet, and he seemed to relax. I guessed it was a load off his back knowing that possessing the machines, making and circulating the counterfeit currency was not going to happen.

He didn't say anything so I continued, "Now here's the thing Suggs. Even though you lusted after those machines, you never had them in your possession. In fact the only thing that you've done that could be held against you by the law is that you shot Newark in the leg and more or less kidnapped him and Bonnie. Newark is not going to go to the cops about being shot, and the cops will probably regard your capturing Bonnie as a good deed. What I'm saying is that you may be able to walk away from this thing now with little or no consequence. If you go killing someone, your life is finished, and from now until the end of it you'll have nothing but regrets. What's it going to be?"

My instincts were correct. Suggs remained quiet for a minute and then looked at me with a hint of kindness in his eyes instead of hate. I could tell the words were hard to say but he got them out. "I was ready to kill everyone to get back at the whole damn system for Gina. But I'm really not that much of a bastard even though I try to be. I hear what you're saying. I know I have nothing to gain by taking this vengeance shit any further. And my group has nothing to gain either since the machines are out of the picture. I'm sorry I got Gina mixed up in it. I didn't know how fuckin' crazy that bitch Bonnie really was until just now. I'll tell you the truth, Caine, I'm sick of the whole militia thing. Every since I've been in it, my life has gone downhill. Gina told me, over and over, that I should get away from those assholes. She was right. I'm gonna do it out of respect for her."

All Suggs ever needed was a good excuse to climb out of the toilet bowl of life he put himself in. Now he had a good reason and he was going for it.

"You just grew up, Suggs. I wish I could take care of smoothing things over about the kidnapping and shooting, but that's a matter for the local fuzz. I'm sure the PD will understand your motivation for bringing those two over here, in light of Gina's death. The shooting could be an accident if Newark sees it that way. You did good getting Bonnie to confess. You ought to consider changing sides Suggs. You got the intimidation thing down pat, and that's a real plus for a cop."

It's too big of a leap to think Suggs would ever be a cop, but maybe he would change his life enough that, in his mind, Gina would be proud of him.

We went back into the room where Newark and Bonnie were tied up. Suggs' entrance got a reaction from Bonnie. She screamed, "Don't kill us! Please don't kill us!"

Suggs replied, "I coulda' done away with you, bitch, but I changed my mind. You're gonna suffer the rest of your life in some dirty-ass prison for what you've done. You're staying tied up here until the law comes for you."

I didn't want to tell Newark or Bonnie about the Secret Service's seizure in San Diego, or that Moshe Zucker, Jr. was hauled off to a federal detainment center in D.C. They would find out through the proper channels at the right time. As far as Newark and Bonnie knew, the machines were still somewhere out there with Kincaid.

To that end I went to Sugg's bedroom area and used his phone to dial Clark. He answered in his usual unhappy sounding manner.

"I thought you'd be gone by now, Caine. What are you waiting for?"

"I don't like to leave loose ends, detective, so I thought I'd go ahead and grab Bonnie Bliss and Newark for you before leaving, which will be tomorrow afternoon. And by the way, Bonnie made a full confession to me in front of Leon Suggs and Newark. She was blackmailing Martin, and like I thought, he got cold feet and she shot him. She found out by listening to the transmitter under Nelson's desk that Gina was blabbing everything she knew to me, and she shot her. By the way, Detective, that transmitter is still under Nelson's desk."

I could hear Clark's teeth gnashing before I continued, "She admitted taking Nelson's twenty-five caliber pistol from his desk and putting it back after killing Gina. I'll give you a signed statement or a recorded statement of everything she told me. I'm sure Suggs will do the same. Bonnie and Newark are tied up in Suggs' place in Pillar Point. Come and get'em. Suggs and I will wait for you."

There was a pause before Clark answered. "God damn it, Caine, do you try to make me look incompetent on purpose, or is it just your way?"

"The bad guys needed to be brought in and I had the opportunity. You can't fault me for that."

Clark was irritated that I had found Bonnie and Newark. I didn't tell him that Suggs was the one who really grabbed them. I supposed that bit of information would make itself known in the near future. Since Suggs' only overtly illegal act was to shoot Newark in the leg, I wanted to leave him out of it as much as possible.

After giving Clark directions, I hung up and the four of us sat quietly until two Sheriff's cars and Clark's private unmarked car roared down the wharf. Bonnie and Newark were put in separate cars. When Clark found out that Suggs had taken Bonnie and Newark against their will, and shot Newark in the process, he cuffed Suggs and shoved him in the back of his car. It was possible that Suggs could be charged with assault with a deadly weapon and given a federal rap for kidnapping. On top of that, it was a sure bet that he didn't have a permit to carry the gun, let alone have a silencer on it. A big no-no in California.

However, with Suggs, there were mitigating circumstances. After all, he had captured a killer and that could get him off the hook, or at least minimize his punishment. Suggs just had a wake-up call that he appeared to be heeding. I'd probably never see the guy again, but if I did, it would be a new Suggs. The old one died today.

Clark took me along to the station where I wrote a statement and signed it in front of him. He thought that would forestall any requirement for me to show up in court. With Bonnie confessing her guilt, there would be no trial and little need, if any, to produce sworn statements. She would be found guilty by her own admission and sentenced by a criminal court judge. If she were lucky, she would spend the rest of her life behind bars. I didn't have any idea what punishment the feds would lay on Nelson, Kincaid, Zucker, Falcon, and Lawrence. I wanted to call John Lewis to inquire, but he wasn't my favorite guy and would likely tell me I had to go through proper channels to get that information. Screw him. I'd get the information from Clark in a month or so, assuming I was still interested.

26

Packing up and checking out of the hotel on the following morning was a feel-good activity. I was anxious to get back to the boat and head on south. It was an unusual departure. There was no one to say goodbye to. Some circle of acquaintances I developed in California. All of them were in jail or dead. I did call Susan to let her know what happened, and that I was on the way back to Florida.

After turning the car in I had close to seventeen-hundred dollars in cash. I had gone through the five hundred Zucker gave me for expenses but had recouped about three hundred from Nelson before they took him away. The point is, that with the fifteen hundred I had left hidden on the boat, I had thirty-two hundred bucks to start my new life, which I now knew would include being a licensed PI.

It was 2:00 a.m. Wednesday morning when the plane landed at the Daytona Beach airport. I retrieved my one bag and was in a cab on the way to the boat yard fifteen minutes after landing.

Anthem had been moved to a slip adjacent to where I had left her. She looked ship shape and ready to go. I didn't realize how much feeling I had for Anthem until I saw her sitting there. Blood, sweat, and tears do that to you. I plugged my heavy extension cord into dockside power, opened her up, turned on some lights and sat down.

Home sweet home. I immediately began to visualize where in the boat I would put a file cabinet and a desk area large enough to hold the new computer and telephone I was going to need in order to conduct case-work business. I knew I was getting ahead of myself but, I was recharged. I turned out the lights and stretched out on my bed thinking about my new Florida-based company, Caine Investigative Services.

I was out on the dock at ten o'clock Wednesday morning. I'd been gone for a week and thought I'd better check in at the boat-yard office before taking my boat out of the slip. The agreement Zucker had penned before I accepted the job and left for California was in my pocket. Hopefully, I wouldn't have to produce it. Earl, the Yard foreman, was in the office. He greeted me warmly.

"Good to see you, Harry. I don't know what you did while you were gone, but word has it you were responsible for getting Zucker, Jr. and a few other guys picked up by the feds for a federal crime. I thought you were through with being a PI. I guess not, right? Did you get the goods on him and a couple other guys?"

"Yeah. It's true. I guess he got a little anxious to get back to New Jersey. He was trying to prove himself to his old man by pulling off a counterfeiting scheme and it backfired on him."

"I never did trust that guy. I always felt bad about it because my feeling was based on the way he looked and acted around the boat yard. I thought he was probably a crook, knowing who his old man is, and now I know for sure. I hope we'll be better off for it. I understand nothing happened to old man Zucker. You know anything about that?"

"I don't know if the old man was involved or not. But with his reputation and background I doubt if the feds will be able to hang anything on him."

"You're probably right. He still has the controlling interest in this boat yard, so we're all wondering about junior's replacement. Time will tell. You ready to take your boat outa' here?"

Earl could have asked me many more questions, but he didn't. I said, "Yeah, that's why I stopped in. I wanted to make sure everything is in order. I'm talking about the bill."

Earl opened a file drawer and pulled out Anthem's folder. He opened the folder and held up the invoice. A large red square stamped 'PAID IN FULL' announced to all that the bill was squared. It was dated two days ago, Monday, the day Zucker was picked up by the feds. Like I said to Newark a few days ago, I did my job. It appeared that Zucker's last official act at the boat yard was to honor that fact.

EPILOGUE

On my way south from Daytona Beach I found a small marina at the north side of Palm Beach, called the Boat Hook Marina. A retired Miami cop runs it. I liked the way the place looked. I could tell I'd have a good rapport with the management, I felt comfortable, and so I'm still here. There is a nearby inlet from the ocean that gives me an easy out to the ocean, if I should want to take a jaunt to the Bahamas.

I contacted Clark shortly after settling in at my new berth to let him know where he could reach me. It turned out that Bonnie made a full confession to the cops that coincided with my signed statement. He let me know that I wouldn't be needed back in San Mateo County. I wasn't unhappy about that.

I received my Florida PI license two months after arriving at the Boat Hook Marina. The Florida licensing authority verified my many years of experience as a California licensed investigator and licensed me with no hassles.

Shortly thereafter, I received a call from Clark. He told me Nelson had received six months for conspiring to defraud the Federal Government. His license to practice law was suspended for five years. It turns out that the California Bar Association frowns on members who engage in counterfeiting activities, their liberalism notwithstanding.

Kincaid got two years for intent to defraud and for possession of counterfeit currency with intent to distribute.

Just as I predicted, Bonnie was given a life sentence for the two murders, with no possibility of parole. She is serving her time in a woman's facility near Visalia, California.

Suggs was given three years probation due to the fact that what he had done was considered to be in the interest of justice. He and Newark claimed the leg shooting was an accident.

Newark was given a year for conspiracy to defraud the Federal Government and three years for violation of the RICCO Act. His rap sheet worked against him. Clark figured Newark would be out in eighteen months.

Zucker, Falcon and Lawrence each received five years for intent to defraud and for the theft of U.S. currency paper. Lawrence apparently ratted out Falcon, who in turn ratted out Zucker. Who said there was honor among thieves? Clark told me the Secret Service put the clamps on any information regarding the paper theft at ENARC.

That was interesting news, but the important reason for Clark's call was to refer me to an attorney friend of his in Palm Beach whom he thought might give me an assignment. I reevaluated my feelings about Clark. I acted on the referral and, like it was planned, I landed my first assignment as a Florida PI. That was six months and many cases ago.

    One last bit of information; Anne tracked me down to let me know she was planning a trip to Palm Beach. Could life get any better?